143

LOVE ACCORDING TO MUSIQ

Musiq

First published by ***DIP Publishing House*** 06/25/2012

ISBN: 978-1-937182-21-2

Written by: *Musiq Soulchild*

Editor-In-Chief: *Argus O. Milton*

Contents

DEDICATION — 6

INTRO — 7

ACT I: LOVING ME — 10
"The Act of loving yourself"

DEDICATION
"1 4 3"

This book is dedicated to anyone, anywhere in search of real love – be forever encouraged, keep the faith and know that you will find it because you are worthy and deserve every bit of this beautiful and awesome joy of life.
— Musiq Soulchild

INTRO

I know what you're probably thinking; "Who gave Musiq the *right* to *write* a book on love?" or how about this; "Just because he's written songs about love doesn't mean that he can *TELL ME* about love". Well, let me respond by letting everyone know that this book, "143: Love According To Musiq", is simply one person's take on love and what I hope *"you"* the reader could stand to gain from the information inside. In the end, my ultimate goal is to help two people, who are in love or on their way, build a stronger connection – *and* in order to do that I address three main steps to accomplishing this throughout the book:

- **ACT I (Loving ME):** Act I is all about loving yourself. I find that before you can truly love another person you must first love yourself, and furthermore, understand the problems that come with NOT loving yourself while trying to love someone else. When a person is missing something on the inside they make poor decisions and even worse, mistake the wrong things for love. This is why most relationships fail when they face money problems, differences in desires, opinions, and other roadblocks. It doesn't matter what blessings come your way as a couple if individually you're incomplete. When the foundation of each person is unstable, it's only a matter of time before a not so good situation exposes the truth.

- **ACT II (Loving YOU):** In Act II I discuss the dynamics of loving another person, which is only possible when you are whole on the inside. I mean don't get me wrong, I know that most people in relationships are not whole on the inside, but that doesn't change the truth of the matter... the suffering that comes with emotionally unstable people in relationships. And not to wish anyone wrong, but don't expect lasting happiness if your happiness is based on shallow and material representations of love. That house or car he or she bought for you are cool, but what happens if, god forbid, you lose them? What happens when the security and comfort of your life is threatened by job loss or illness? It's easy to say what we think is the "*best*" response but reality has shown us a less than pleasant response to these kinds of obstacles in relationships.

- **ACT III (Loving US):** The lesson of Act III brings together both Act I and II and focuses on the overall relationship. When you can love yourself and your partner without any restrictions, conditions or limitations, the situation will be much more productive and fulfilling for the both of you. I like to compare a good love relationship to a sturdy house... If you build your home on quicksand it will eventually sink no matter what you do, but if you replace the quicksand with concrete the house won't go anywhere. And just like that house, your commitment will rest on something solid... ready to withstand whatever challenges may and will come.

I liken this book to a medical exam. When you go to the doctor for a physical, they don't just check out your arms or your toes to determine if you're healthy. They draw blood, tap on muscles, listen to your heart, ask questions, and so on... we've all been there, so maybe now you a have an idea of what to expect. I want you to think of this book as your love physical, and like a good doctor I left no stone unturned. Although I don't claim to be an expert on relationships, I do, however, know more than some about what love is... I mean c'mon, it's my job to know! And when the points are understood and applied the right way, it can work for any situation. The problem with most situations, and not just romantic relationships, is that there is a lack of basic and fundamental love and appreciation. Whether it's for your job, your car, your clothes, your life... it doesn't matter. We all know that a lack of love will prevent you from doing your very best. It will diminish the quality of any and everything you do. So if nothing else, I want to focus on love, because when the love is right, everything else will fall into place.

ACT I

LOVING ME

If you don't love yourself, then how can you expect to be loved by or love someone else... are you really in love... is there something in your way of true love... do you even know what love means... all these questions and more will be discussed, right here in......

CHAPTER

LOVE

What it IS and is NOT

What Is It?

If I were to ask ten random people – *"what do you think love is"*, I would probably get ten different answers. And by different I am not talking about the words used to describe love, but the entire perception of it altogether according to each person. While one person may base it on actions, another may measure it by words, so it's very important to pay extra close attention, because you just might be with someone for reasons *other* than love. Now, I can't tell you what to believe or whether or not your feelings are real... but what I *can* tell you is that way too often so many things are mistaken for love, and it's only when the relationship falls apart do those things become so obvious. This is exactly how people find themselves in situations that are based on the wrong things, something that just doesn't feel right. The thing about the word love is that it sounds and feels good to say, which is how and why it's often abused, and if you've ever had that word spoken to you then you know just how easily it can sweep you up.

What Love is <u>Not</u>

I don't claim to know everything about love, nor am I here to dictate to you or anyone else about it. However, I do understand what love is *not*, and with that I can help to make some sense of it for those who don't. A good starting point to answering this question is to ask yourself; "what is my love based on?" The goal here is to see whether or not your "love" relationship is out of balance with only your benefit in mind. A one sided situation will never work. This is important because true love doesn't begin with you. Not to be confused with having love and respect for yourself – that's a different part of your journey and should come before ever attempting, or expecting, to truly love in a relationship. Otherwise you will confuse love with a vain pursuit to satisfy only your desires instead of creating a mutually fulfilling experience. You will always look for the payback or material representation of what you think is love, which will only cause problems, for instance:

Confusion –

It's really easy to become confused when talking about love, because there are so many different gestures to represent our love. Gestures are nice and can be very effective in communicating how you feel about someone, however, they should never be mistaken for love itself. When this happens it's only a matter of time before problems follow. This is why people who thought they were in love all of a sudden believe that they fell out of love – when the reality is that they were never in love to begin with. Knowing love for what it truly is will save you years of wasted time and headache. You can easily find yourself caught up in a vicious cycle for the rest of your life... or, you can learn **what love is not** and avoid going down that road.

Musiq

Have you ever considered what love means to you? Ask yourself; what are my requirements for love… does a person have to make a certain amount of money or some other loveless factor for you to want them? Not saying that you shouldn't have standards or ignore red flags – because you might end up starting a family with this person, and if you already have children you want to choose very carefully who you bring into the picture. So please don't take this as if I'm saying you should bring just anyone around and then when they turn out to be crazy blame Musiq… no no, let's not do that. I do believe that being selective is being smart. Furthermore, don't get stuck pointing fingers either, because it's just as important to find the red flags in yourself as it is the other person.

Chaos –

The reason so many marriages and relationships don't last, in my opinion, is because of a weak foundation. And by foundation I'm talking about *you* individually. Before you can have a good relationship with anyone else, you have to first build one with yourself. There's no way around it, you have to deal with the person in the mirror – It's pretty much like being in a relationship with yourself. Fall in love with you FIRST! Answer this; how can you expect anyone to love you, if *you* don't even love you? And you have to do more than just believe that you love yourself – you have to know it. And the only way to know it, is to know who you are and then accept it. If not you will spend your entire life trying to become something that you think is worth loving and nine times out of ten that something won't be you.   Find out what is holding you back and remove it.   What you lack within will always manifest externally, so no need to act surprised when the drama starts.   When looking for that special someone your "checklist" will be corrupted if you have unresolved issues within.   If the inside isn't right your decisions will be vulnerable to the needs of your problems, which is not love at all.   Your problem could be greed, vanity, insecurities, or any number of issues.   So naturally, when choosing a partner the emptiness within will guide the process and aim to satisfy the void, which is only temporary until that person no longer does it for you anymore.   So my point is this, once the empty purpose has run its course, the inevitable divorce or separation *will* follow.   Some couples try their best to hold on because they don't want to let other people down, or hurt the kids, or whatever the reason, not realizing that more damage is being done than good.

What Love Is

Love, in *my* observation, is a culmination of many… many things. Most of us perceive it as a solitary emotion, when in reality its home to so many others. Love is multidimensional, and consists of various emotions like compassion, respect, loyalty, understanding, forgiveness, consideration, honor, trust, protection, and so forth. So you

15

see, when a person begins to understand what it means to love they will inevitably take it more seriously. And when your mode of operation is motivated by love, it's very unlikely that you would choose to live by or do anything for any other reason, especially if it could jeopardize your relationship(s). I didn't want to talk about love in the same way that everyone else does, because it's going to take more than just a good write up to repair how love has been misrepresented – in our hearts, minds, and most importantly our relationships. And this goes for inside the home as well as outside. A deeper understanding is necessary as we find ourselves with more reasons to fall out of love than to remain in it. How can anyone expect to experience a truly meaningful relationship without first dealing with the problems that stand in the way? Honestly... I feel that we all know what love is, because it's already within us... the problem here, as I said before, is when things that are *not* love take over and are mistaken for it. Just think of love as your steel armor, when used the right way, it will provide you with all the protection needed to survive. But when you replace it with steel painted cardboard, there's only so much protection it can give. So when using this cardboard, which looks just like the real thing, it'll only hold-up for a quick second in the face of trouble before it gives out, and you'll inevitably end up getting your heart broken or breaking someone else's. So now, my question to you is – how strong is your armor?

Love Failed

I've heard it so many times; "Love Failed", when the truth is that love never fails.... and before you argue the point let me clarify what I mean. The sad reality is that most people get together for many reasons other than the right ones. And I'm not just talking about the obvious such as money or looks, no – there are all sorts of reasons people hook up in error and believe that it's love. Let's say you meet a wonderful person and they make you feel extremely good about yourself. Let's stop right there – without going any further into the example I can tell you where things went wrong. The unfortunate reality is that relationships that fail were already doomed from the start. If you need a man or woman to feel good about yourself... I repeat... if you NEED, *key word* "need", a man or woman to feel good about yourself, then the problem is just that, yourself – and sadly most people don't even see themselves as *"the"* problem, instead they'd rather point fingers at everybody else. The fact that you *"need"* someone to make you feel good about yourself means that you were incomplete before they ever came along. This is what I mean by mistaking love for other things. A void inside has you in search of validation through the confirmation and acceptance of others. You might not even like this person but still choose to be with them because of the way they make you feel. But the moment this "oh so special" person slips up and drops the ball, even if it's just one time, you begin to lose faith in how you think and feel about them.

17

Then of course you blame them while the true problem escapes behind the pointed finger, your finger. This is a big reason behind why so many relationships fail. When things are done right from the start better decisions are made, and therefore you get much better outcomes. If you have unresolved issues then you should do something about it, right now, before getting serious with anyone. You can ignore it if you want but don't be upset when it comes back around to bite you. No one person is the same and therefore every situation is unique. Whoever you go to for advice, whether it be a friend, pastor, or counselor, do what is best for your journey. True love is a beautiful thing and everyone deserves to experience it.

Are we really in love?

The question; whether or not you are loved, is a fair question and there is nothing wrong with asking it. But when you ask yourself this question I hope that you are looking for the right confirmation. Although material things are fun and can be very sweet gestures of love, they should never be looked to for true confirmation of love. This doesn't mean that you should stop with the gestures... it's always nice to receive and give gifts, but there may come a time when those things don't come as often or at all – does this mean you aren't loved? – *never mind... I'll answer that for you* – of course not. And if his/her behavior does change, whatever the reason behind it should be recognized and if legitimate, accepted. If a person's motives are bad,

18

then it's just that, they're bad. Identify the red flags and go from there. It's just as important to know where *you* stand when it comes to love also. If you're expecting love, then you should also be sure that you are ready and willing to give it. And I don't want to give off the impression that just because someone makes you feel better about your insecurities that your love is not real, but you should be aware that if you have to depend on somebody else to feel good about yourself, trouble isn't far away. And maybe at the beginning you did get with someone because they were more stable than yourself, or something along those lines. I mean, the truth of the matter is that we select partners who we feel will compliment us. And that reason could be financial stability or a boost in confidence, and this is neither right nor wrong, it's just what it is. The problem comes in when your only reason behind pursuing and holding on to someone is shallow and based on material things.

EXAMPLE: PART 1 (TWO PEAS WITH A PROB)

Monica turns off the television in a rage and slings the remote across the room.

"These damn fools on television can't seem to appreciate a woman unless she looks like a damn Super Model!"

She says as she turns to her friend in search of a response. Monica stomps across the room and into the bathroom and slams the door behind her. Her friend, Kimberly, takes a deep breath and falls backwards onto the bed. Staring at the ceiling she begins thinking about Monica's comment. As a close friend, Kimberly was somewhat of a sounding board for Monica. She was all too familiar with Monica's position on how society encourages people to like some things and dislike others. This particular incident came after a certain rap artist boasted about his "light skinned" girl as if brown skin was not good enough – while on the other hand Kimberly, a Caucasian brunette with brown eyes, has also expressed her frustration with the way white women with blond hair and blue eyes are praised so much. And although neither Monica or Kimberly see themselves as better than anyone else, they both have a common dislike for those who single out a set group of people and label them as "better". After several minutes Monica exits the bathroom looking like a million bucks. Her well curved frame is complimented by a black fitted skirt that stops a few inches above the knee. Her C-cup breasts sit up in perfect union as she reaches down to fasten the ankle straps of her five inch heels.

"How do I look?" A smiling Monica asks while fidgeting impatiently as she awaited her friend's response.

"You look sexy girl, who's the lucky man?" says Kimberly

"Oh, just some guy I met last weekend at the supermarket while waiting in line. He had the sexiest voice and swag for life! He made his way through like ten people in a long line just to get to me!"

"Oh yeah?"

"Yup, sure did. Now let one of these fools on television tell me I don't look good!"

Monica makes her way to the other room where her daughter, three year old Kyra, was sleeping. She leans over and kisses her on the forehead. Tiptoeing out the door she waves bye to Kimberly who was babysitting for the night.

CHAPTER

COMMUNICATION

Words vs. Actions

No matter how you look at it, every relationship will experience some bumps on the road to love. If you're looking for a relationship without challenges then you're looking for something that doesn't exist. I believe that challenges are the best teachers and you shouldn't run from them... in fact, instead of dreading them you should welcome them. I say this because challenges offer opportunities to fix what is broken. So actually, a little bump here and there, when looked upon positively, can be very constructive. The real problem comes from a lack of communication, or rather a clash in styles when it comes to communication between men and women. Because our styles are so different, if left unchecked, the friction between the two can create big problems and threaten a relationship. This is why having at least a basic understanding is so important when it comes to connecting with that special someone. And this doesn't mean expecting them to communicate exactly the way you do – focus on gaining an understanding of their natural mode of communication. Not everyone is the same when it comes to this – some people are better at it than others. However, as far as the fundamental differences go between the sexes, they're inescapable and should always be respected by both sides. And whether or not you're willing to open up, learn, and appreciate those differences will have everything to do with the success of your relationship(s).

WORDS: What Are You Saying?

So what can be done about the natural differences between sexes when it comes to communication? Well... nothing. And I don't mean to downplay it, *nor* am I saying that you should accept a lack of communication. What I mean by "nothing" is accepting the fact that men and women are simply different in this department. Ladies, yes... a man *should* listen to you, yes he *should* be concerned about the way you feel, however, you shouldn't automatically associate the way he chooses to expresses himself with not caring. And fellas... just know that women generally appreciate a greater level of feedback than many of you are willing to give. Everyone has to give up something, so come out of your gender-shells and do what's best for the relationship. If you need clarification on what a person's actions mean... then try asking instead of assuming the worst. When someone is unwilling to communicate or work through a problem in a relationship, then that's something entirely different – and something the two of you will have to work out before any real communication can take place. When you don't factor in the differences between men and women in this area, you find yourself with expectations that can be very unrealistic to the situation. Either it's; *"she talks and complains too much!"*, or *"he just doesn't understand me!".* When these types of attitudes take over you accomplish very little if anything at all, because the focus will be all wrong. If just one of you has the right idea and tries to communicate the right way, I'm sorry but that just won't be enough.

ACTIONS: What Are You Doing?

Communication is more than just words, and when done right it has nothing at all to do with yelling or being overly dramatic. When communicating with that special someone you have to be fair in assessing the situation, taking into account the history of your relationship to best determine the implications of the other person's actions, I repeat... ***taking into account the history of your relationship to best determine the implications of the other person's actions.*** Do **NOT** allow momentary amnesia to take over, causing you to forget who you're dealing with when you find yourself all worked up over something that more than likely means absolutely nothing in the grand scope of things. Look... you're not going to like everything that this person does, however, it would be crazy to *not* consider this person's track record. Ask yourself; Is this something that consistently happens or just a simple mistake? And yes, believe it or not mistakes do happen more than once, but even still *all* factors should be considered. If a person works three jobs and forgets to load the dishwasher once or twice a week, then I think that just comes with the territory. You want to always look for the meaning behind the action. Ask yourself; what does this mean as it relates to "*us*". When you do this you'll realize that more times than not you're overreacting. Either the person you're with cares about you or they don't... it's that simple. When you look at the actions of the other person, do so from a spectrum of past to present. If the behavior consistently shows that you guys are on different pages, then you have a choice to make. If you decide to overlook the obvious red flags then **you** become the one to blame. Failure to confront and deal with the situation will only keep the problem alive. By not making the sometimes tough decision to separate yourself from the situation, your message will not be taken seriously, no matter how much complaining you do. You must be willing to walk away if your feelings are not important enough to be respected and given some attention.

INTENTIONS: Behind, Under & Between

Reading between the lines is crucial in the jungle of love, especially with so many people out for the wrong things. Knowing what words and actions from that *"special someone"* really mean will save you much time and energy that could otherwise be spent on the right person. You must also be accountable and honest with yourself and not close your eyes to obvious signs of caution. Now... in the defense of many, there are people out there with some serious game who can easily slip past your radar. But even if they do make it through, the red flags will eventually come. And your job then is to be real about the situation and make a decision or shut up and deal with it. Once the red flags are present and you choose to stay, it becomes *your* choice to suffer. And yes I know that sometimes weeding out the nonsense is easier said than done. You would think that some people made a career out of running game... and most of us know them as "Player", "Golddigger" and of course "Big Pimpin"... pimpin since been pimpin since been... you know the rest.   But it's only because they are ever so very clever with their game that they can remain under the radar for so long.   When someone clings to another person for the wrong reasons, it's most likely because they have something to lose if the other person leaves.   Or in other words they're getting *"something"* out of the relationship that they otherwise would not have. Whether that something is a place to crash, money to have, love to make – or sex to get, their motive is solely what they can get from you and once that need is replaced... guess what... *"IIIIII'm sorry but your services are no longer needed, have a nice rest of your life!"*

Although there is no one way to know what a person's true intentions are, nine times out of ten you can know by comparing words to actions over time, and then cross referencing them against different situations. I'm not saying that you should get all technical and setup a monitoring station to keep track of what someone is doing... *please don't, no one is worth the time or money*... but if the need arises you should know what to look for:

• **Questions vs. Reasoning:** This is assuming that you have given them the full benefit of the doubt, therefore not overreacting and giving you a real reason to look deeper. Maybe it's been three years and no talk of marriage, or maybe you've noticed a change in their behavior.

• **Reasoning vs. Communication:** There just might be a good reason behind why things are the way that they are. And you should hear those reasons out without judgment or accusing them of something your mind came up with to explain their actions. Of course you want to take into account your history with this person in addition to any red flags – *not* wanting to look stupid is not a justification for being unfair.

• **Communication vs. Action:** Listen to what is being said compared to what is being done. What did he/she say when you asked about taking your relationship to the next level? What did he/she do about the situation that was supposed to be fixed after you both talked about it? I know that some things may take a little longer to compare than others depending on what they are. What you are doing here is simply aligning actions with words. If it quacks like a duck then it's probably a duck!

• *Actions vs. Consistency:* Okay, to be fair let's say that once or twice the words and actions did not exactly match. You have to give each situation its own look, because no one situation is the same and therefore actions can carry very different meanings. For example, if we're talking about a couple with children, married or not, and the problem is that one parent is forgetting to pick the kid(s) up from school – that carries a much different weight than say a person getting a takeout order wrong. These two situations have different consequences in the event something does go wrong. If some random person just happens to wander along and grabs the kid(s) that's a problem – but not getting a bag of chips with your sandwich won't hurt anything but your feelings.

• **Consistency vs. Circumstance:** Whether or not communication at this point is needed to see the truth behind the situation is a case by case call. You will have to make this call according to what you have determined overall. Once you have made clear your expectations, *within reason*, and the other person is unwilling to meet you at least half way – then it's your call on whether or not to accept it. In the end, no matter what is said, if the words are not supported by actions, then they carry no value.

IMAGINATION: You Didn't See Anything

Sometimes reading too much into things can work against you. I've seen women time and time again come up with their own version of how a man feels about them, or whether or not he is being good to her. Like I said before, either a person loves you or they don't. Don't go finding reasons to add drama to your relationship. You don't have to be unhappy or make problems... REALLY... you don't... so don't get caught up in creating them. Unfortunately some people only feel alive in a relationship when there is tension and chaos – when the reality, more times than not, is that their fuel for being in a relationship is not love but something else entirely... *we talked about this last chapter*. The point is that there will be times where you may feel a person's actions don't exactly match what you hoped them to be – however, any action is better than no action. Of course you don't want to accept actions intended to pacify you for the moment, but you will know with time whether their actions are sincere or not!

Compromise is Caring –

Men, you should always remember that women like to hear things. So if you truly feel something for them, then why not express it? And I know how some of you might feel about this, I for one am a little conflicted when it comes to saying words just because she wants to "hear" them. This is why it's so easy to run game on many females. And I'm not implying that women are idiots or so naïve that they're unable to spot *bullsh_t* when it's being served – no, not at all – I just know how much women can cling to words, especially when they are really into a man. And there's something else that has always puzzled me... when a man does a million and one things to express how he feels for a woman – yet a word that doesn't necessarily mean anything is appreciated so much more. Of course this isn't the case with all women, but for those of you who fit the profile please stop it, because if you're not careful it can cause a man to lose his motivation when it comes to doing special things for you. And no, this is not a threat from men so please don't take it that way. It's just something you may want to keep in mind!

Now men – If time is the issue in your relationship, then do what you can in response to her concern. If your time is limited, that's fine, perhaps you could call or text a little more, or maybe on the weekends or whenever your schedule opens up, make a little less time for other things and give it to the woman who you claim to love. Regardless of your situation, if you care about her and your relationship, then you should want to fix what is broken before it becomes a real problem.

Help Me, Help You –

Ladies, you can really help your man *and* your relationship in many ways here. The first to mention is patience and understanding, especially if you **know** that he's doing his best. Another is to speak your mind clearly concerning what you need from him – and yes, **it's that simple!** If you want your man to spend more time with you, then just say so, find a way to put it on his radar – but don't blow up on him in the process. I know some of you women may think to yourself "*why should I have to convince this grown ass man to spend time with his woman, if he loves me like he says he does then he'll **make** the time!*"... am I right?......*be honest*.. I'm RIGHT, right? Look, the reality is that most men are going to be preoccupied with other things in one way or another, and when a man is focused on something he can be pretty terminal about it, and often times at the expense of your emotions. Ladies, we don't mean any harm by it, we just may need a gentle nudge every now and then to get things back on track with you, that's all, so unless you *"know"* that it's in fact something else, please don't take it so personal. For example... don't just get mad 'cause he ain't doing what you want him to do, and instead of giving him a chance to do anything about it you just "**go in**" on him and take out all of your frustration – *not* realizing that he has NO idea where this is coming from, and therefore naturally he's going to look at you as though you're trippin'... meanwhile no real progress is ever made.

Being Honest with Yourself –

If the nature of your relationship wasn't ever established, then you shouldn't hold it against the other person when things don't go exactly the way you wanted them to. No matter who you are, your intentions should be made clear upfront, or as soon as possible. If you don't let people know what you are looking for then there is bound to be some confusion and this is yet another way feelings get hurt. On the flipside, if you *ARE* clear about your intentions and what you expect and the other person is on a different page, then basically you have to decide whether *you* should leave this person alone *or* adjust, adapt, and figure it out. Choosing to be naïve to the reality of your situation will not change or help anything. You cannot make a person want you *nor* can you mold them into what you want them to be. Sure you might be able to give advice on how to do things differently whether it be dressing or cleaning up, but that means very little for you if your relationship goals aren't the same.

Musiq

Keep Your Options Open –

Until you know exactly what the other person wants, it is important to keep your options open. This is a mistake made by so many people, getting caught up in trying to force a person's hand. Even if you get them to bend, if their heart isn't into it, it will only be a matter of time before they want out. It's a big gamble to be with someone who is unable to appreciate you by their own free will. All this will do is keep your partner, who you claim to love and only want to be happy, from ever truly being so. Furthermore, you will also block *yourself* from finding the right person for you. So right here, right now, I am asking you... please do not sell yourself short by chasing a person who doesn't ***appreciate you for who you are***, as you are. When you keep your options open, the right person can find and connect with you, giving you both a real chance at happiness and true love.

EXAMPLE: PART 2 (I THINK I LOVE HIM)

(A text conversation between Monica & Kimberly)

॰ıll *L&M*　　　　　　*1:43*　　　　　

> **Kim:** Hey girl
> **Kim:** What are you up to?
> **Monica:** nuthin, bout to go out again
> **Kim:** With that one guy, what was his name?
> **Monica:** Sam, and yes I'm going out with him, he's so sweet
> **Monica:** and I know it's only been a couple weeks but I think I love him
> **Kim:** LMAO!
> **Kim:** What?
> **Kim:** Already?!?
> **Monica:** why are you laughing...
> **Monica:** ain't you supposed to be with me on this
> **Kim:** Yeah i know but damn Monica...
> **Kim:** Didn't you say you just met this boy, how can you be SOOO sure????
> **Monica:** you wasn't there, so you don't know..
> **Monica:** you don't know how he makes me feel
> **Monica:** i think i just found the 1
> **Kim:** Come on Monica, you know you my girl and I love you right..
> **Kim:** Right??
> **Kim:** Girl whatever, I just don't want you to get hurt, that's all!
> **Monica:** I know u tryna look out for me, but I just need u to trust me on this
> **Kim:** Well, if you need me girl you know that I'm here for you
> **Monica:** of course baby cakes, that's all i wanted you to say!
> **Kim:** wow..
> **Monica:** nah, I'm just playing..
> **Monica:** you know i know you've always been there for me and I appreciate that!

CHAPTER

INSECURITIES

Bringing Old Baggage to New Love

Your Worst Enemy

Insecurities have a way of turning people into animals. And when they strike they come fast and hard, showing little respect for the other person and sometimes permanently damaging relationships. If you've ever fell victim to this very powerful emotion then you know exactly what it feels like, and more importantly how it hurts everyone involved. And if you've ever been guilty of it – *you know who you are* – then you know firsthand how strong the wave can be. Look, the reality of it is this; no one is completely secure no matter who you are or how much money you have, insecurities are always just right around the corner. Unfortunately this is very normal and you shouldn't beat yourself up over it. The real problem is when you allow insecurity to take over and lose all control. When this happens some very fine lines can be crossed. In the pit of insecurity the situation becomes all about you. Think about the self gratifying feeling of selfishness that you felt, and how whatever you said or did seemed to make you feel better. An insecure person might say whatever comes to their mind, no matter how cruel, in the name of getting you back for hurting them – even if it means making the other person, *the one you claim to love... remember* – feel bad. You must keep in mind that in the end this problem, *your* problem, will only get worse. But most people don't realize this until it is too late.

37

Musiq

PREVIOUS CATS

Previouscatsyndrome: Holding the new person in your life accountable for what happened, or what someone *else* may have done to you, in a previous relationship.

Insecurities are the result of a lack of trust and faith, not only in the person that you're with but also within yourself. Think of it as a self centered belief system gone wrong. And when someone acts in a way *opposite* of your belief system, the typical response is to become insecure. The presence of the emotion is mostly normal, however, when accompanied by the "Previous Cats Syndrome"... male or female... it mutates, and more times than not rationale goes out the window. Everything that someone else did to you is then attached to the actions of the current person, so I cannot stress enough how important it is to...

DEAL WITH YOUR PAST BEFORE MOVING FORWARD WITH YOUR LIFE!!!

Of course life goes on, but relationships end, so for your own sake and the person coming into your life, you must let the past go before entertaining another commitment. I am NOT saying that you should be stupid and throw caution to the wind, because you'll only succeed at proving that you haven't learned anything, and therefore destined to repeat your past mistakes. For example: a duck is a duck, however... a duck is also a bird, and so is an eagle, so would you hold it against the eagle if it started to fly... just because it reminds you of the duck? My point is, ladies and gentlemen, if the new person in your life is doing what the last person who hurt you did, it would be foolish of you to ignore it.   Using what you have learned from past experiences is not being insecure, that's just being smart. Insecurity is altogether a different thing, and many undeserving people find themselves at the mercy of its wrath. It isn't fair, or safe for the matter, to assume that the new person in your life is going to make the same mistakes as the previous one. This is a mistake first of all because it's not at all true. People hurt other people every day, both women and men. And not to be insensitive to anyone's situation, but being honest about the fact that it can happen to anyone, including you, puts you in the driver's seat. Now, where you end up totally depends on how far you allow it to go.

Getting Trust Back

Trust is something that I feel has to be earned, maintained, and honored. Not that you should give every person who enters your life the third degree, however, being observant and getting to know someone is just a part of the process. It doesn't matter whether or not they have a shaky track record. What's important is how you go about trusting the person you're with. I don't think making them feel as if they are under the gun is the right way to do it. There is no need for the new person in your life to be threatened, directly or indirectly, by what you might do or "cut off" if they ever cheated on you... hint, hint. Not only is that inappropriate but also shows emotional instability. So go ahead... if you want to scare someone away just let your neurosis run point in your relationship, and *see how they run!* Too many people go looking for problems where often times there aren't any to find. One thing you should remember is that if there is a problem it will eventually surface. Putting yourself through hell by creating "*what if*" scenarios in your mind is so very unnecessary, and can be extremely dangerous! If you've invited someone into your life, then it's kind of unfair to not give them a fair shake. If for whatever reason you feel that they don't deserve one then why are you with them? You can only blame someone else so much before *you* become the one to blame.

The Privacy Policy

Privacy is something that changes over time, losing its grip as a commitment deepens and relinquishes the need or desire for it. For people in deep, meaningful, and soul fulfilling relationships, there tends to be less of a need for privacy – however, completely abandoning privacy, regardless of the relationship, I would say is very rare. Even after years of being together there are some areas where privacy should not be lost. And this could be anything from a person's phone activity or showing up places unannounced, and a whole list of other things. And it's not so much about you being kept in the dark about things, but more so a matter of respecting the other person's personal space. Commitment or not, it's healthy for a person to have some kind of a life outside of their relationship. Of course every relationship is different because people are different. What may work for one might be unthinkable for another. Whatever the case, I think that boundaries and rules should be established upfront when it comes to privacy. Not respecting another's privacy can lead to unnecessary problems, especially early on in a relationship.

When YOU become the problem

I know that some of you have good reason to question the person in your life. Maybe they've cheated or told a big lie and you can't seem to get past it. But no matter what reasons exist for your current state of distrust and overall fear, there are always two sides to a story. And at the end of it, if someone makes you so unhappy there is only so much blaming available *from* you before the blame falls *on* you. It's never okay to breach a promise of trust, whether you call it cheating or being unfaithful – I don't want anyone to believe that I feel otherwise. However, knowing when *you've* become the problem is the difference between accountability and excuses, so let's talk about this. I think it should be kept simple and straight to the point – remember, either a person wants to build something with you or they don't. When it comes to all of the drama surrounding relationships, my philosophy is simple: **DROP IT** or **DROP EM'**... some things are better left alone – and just the same – some people! It's very important to

41

Musiq

remember that there is always a solution. You don't have to live in hell to find love. You don't have to be insecure or jealous, so why go through all the trouble to make yourself that way. There's always an option to diffuse a potentially hostile situation if you're willing to work through it… but, if you don't want to discuss the issue, then go grab yourself a tissue, and leave the other person alone! No one in search of a true and meaningful relationship has the time to throw you a pity party every time you can't have things your way. When you let someone new into your life, give them a chance without all the unnecessary drama. When you don't you run the risk of blocking your relationship from growing and keeping yourself stuck in your own mess. Now on the other hand, if you've been given good reason to doubt a person's commitment, you should act wisely and do what you must. Being cautious is not the problem, nor is it your problem if someone can't seem to do right by you. Problems come when being cautious preoccupies your mind and everything the other person does falls suspect.

EXAMPLE: PART 3 (0-2-60)

It's been over a month since Monica's exit from her previous relationship. Although things were promising in the beginning, her insecurities and inability to fully trust anyone caused a huge conflict in her situation with Sam, which essentially led to their relationship's demise. And even though the pain is still fresh, she decides to open up once again. Ironically, she meets another gentleman by the name of Brian at the same store where she met Sam. She briefly wonders to herself if this was a sign to leave him alone or not. Giving no real attention to the idea that the coincidence meant trouble, she agrees to see him, and then see him again. A week or so later they meet up at a restaurant for dinner. She is surprised by his manners and gentlemanly ways and just knows that something must be off........it *has* to be. Outside of telling her that she looks great, he makes little to no comments about her body – which by the way was a sight to see. With arguably one of the best figures in the world, she wore a loose fitting dress that draped over her perfect physic flattering every curve in ways impossible to imagine while still maintaining high class. To her amazement and dismay, she was surprised that he wasn't looking for ways to climb all over her. Monica wondered to herself whether or not he was gay or just trying to run some reverse psychology type game on her. At the end of the night he takes her home and walks her to the door. They hug and he leaves. The next day

Musiq

Monica, both cheerful and skeptical, tells Kimberly about her date. Kimberly is happy that things went so well and encourages her to go out again despite her skepticism.

(Monica grabs her phone and texts Kimberly)

L&M　　　　　　*1:43*　　　　　

> Monica: hey girl
> Kim: Heeeyyy!!!
> Kim: Sooooooo, how did it gooooo???
> Monica: it was cute
> Kim: Okaaayyy???
> Monica: i mean he was nice and romantic, u kno a real gentlemen
> Monica: totally into me and wasn't tryina get me in bed all fast
> Kim: Oop..
> Monica: what?
> Kim: Ohhh monica, poor sweet innocent monica
> Monica: what!!!
> Kim: i think that's called gay
> Monica: girl shut up, he ain't gay
> Monica: omg you are so dumb sometimes
> Kim: Girl look, If a man that fine went out with YOU looking like you did..
> Kim: And wasn't "tryina get you in bed all fast" shhh..
> Kim: IJS, IDK!!!
> Monica: he's not okay, that's what i DO know!!!
> Kim: Alright if you say so, i believe you
> Kim: Ok so now what, you gonna go see him again?
> Monica: I don't know, I mean i like him and everything but..
> Kim: Hey...did you have a good time last night?
> Monica: yeah, i guess i did
> Kim: Then don't think about anything else
> Kim: And forget everything i just said and do it
> Monica: yeah? u really think i should
> Kim: Yeah girl, if he makes you happy, ynot?

Monica agrees and shortly thereafter calls Brian and thanks him for such a wonderful time. As she expected he offers to take her out again and she agrees. They meet the very next night and once again she is impressed by how he treats her. She's convinced that maybe this guy could be someone very special in her life. After several more dates and a month later, Monica and Brian were officially a couple. And although the start of their relationship was very positive, with each day Monica questioned Brian's motives more and more, causing her insecurities to soar through the roof. Eventually her insecurities grew into a monster, leading her to question his attraction for her and accusing him of being into other types of women. Although Brian gave her no reasons at all to accuse him of these things, the trend continued as the situation began to spiral out of control.

(A random text)

 L&M   *1:43*

Monica: hey babe, what you doing
Brian: hey, i was just about to hit you, wasup?
Monica: boy stop no you wasn't, you just saying that cause i texted you first
Brian: ok
Monica: what's that mean
Brian: nothing, just ok
Monica: "O K" if you say so..
Brian: whatever, anyway what you doing later
Monica: why u miss me
Brian: yea, i wanna see you, you gonna be up?
Monica: idk, i gotta get up early
Brian: me too, still wanna see you
Monica: it's okay, u don't have to if u tired
Brian: what are you talking about?

Musiq

Monica: u said u gotta get up early so it's okay
Brian: yea but did you read the rest wut i said
Monica: yea, i did
Brian: so what you saying you don't want me to see you?
Brian: is that it?
Monica: i know u got "allot" goin on so it's cool, ur off the hook for 2nite
Brian: what's that suppose to mean
Monica: whats what suppose to mean
Brian: i got "a lot" goin on so I'm off the hook
Monica: im just saying don't worry you ain't gotta make time for little old me
Brian: wtf
Brian: look i don't know what you talkin about
Brian: matta fact forget it, i holla at you 2moro
Monica: it's all good, i already know
Brian: u already know what?!?
Monica: like i said don't worry about it
Brian: man whatever ur trippin
Brian: am out
Brian: luv u
Brian: g'nite!
Monica: yea, just like i thought, go head and do u then
Monica: it ain't like i can stop u anyway
Monica: bet u ain't gon have me looking crazy out here
Monica: I'm too grown for all this
Monica: betta go find wunna these thirsty ass young chix who think u soooo fine
Monica: i ain't got time to put up with this sh_t
Monica: i got a daughter to think about that depends on ME!
Monica: I promise on her and everything I ain't the one boo boo
Monica: u got me all the way f_cked up best believe that!!!
Monica: hello
Monica: helloooooo...
Monica: so now u gonna ignore me
Monica: wuteva

CHAPTER

REDEMPTION

Love You Once Shame on Me, Hurt Me Twice Shame on You

The Implications

No matter the reason behind a breakup, by giving someone a second chance you're basically saying that they have been forgiven. If people really thought this through there would probably be far less second chances given in relationships. To further stress my point... when most people give second chances they don't really mean it, and what I mean by this is – they will claim to forgive yet never give themselves an opportunity to get past the hurt. So even after years have passed, the incident is still being thrown in the middle of disputes. It's foolish to give someone a second chance yet not give yourself another chance to trust them again. That's crazy, JUST LEAVE! Because if you're not willing to give that person an honest opportunity to redeem themselves it's pointless and you're just wasting everyone's time. And nine times out of ten when this is the case you can't still be in it for love, because love doesn't behave that way. You need to ask yourself "then why am I still here?"... and be honest about it.

The Agreements

So you've come to a decision that you no longer want to be with this person. Maybe they cheated or just didn't live up to your expectations of a relationship. Despite why you left, let's say the other person is stuck on getting you back. All sorts of promises of change are made as they shower you with "I'm sorry" and all sorts of gifts in desperate hopes of winning you back. Fast forward some and you finally give in and decide to try once again with the belief that they've changed.

Okay, first rule of thumb, make sure to be very clear about your expectations moving forward. This will rule out any excuses that may be used if the behavior returns. Now, I think it goes without saying that a second chance is not the same as first hooking up, therefore it automatically comes with a litter extra pressure by way of rules and questions to root out any bad weeds. Depending on your reason for leaving, in the first place, will have everything to do with the new rules. And even though they *were* in the wrong, it's unnecessary and unfair to punish them in ways unrelated to the problem itself. If you leave someone for being too insecure, then you shouldn't treat them as if they cheated on you. Whatever the new rules are it's important that they are followed. If you are the offender, then don't get mad when the other person asks to go through your phone or whatever else. I cannot stress enough the importance of doing what is necessary to regain a person's trust or confidence back. Remember, if someone really wants to be with you and appreciates the second chance given, they should have no problem bending according to the rules in order to reestablish confidence in the relationship.

The Separation

Moving on can be tricky sometimes, depending on your situation and attachment to the person you're involved with. Because of the iffy nature of emotions it can be difficult deciding on whether or not you should let go. If this is you I want you to ask yourself the following questions beginning with; "does this person..."

- Cause suffering for you?

- Bring out the worst in you?

- Refuse to do right by you?

Sometimes in order to make the necessary and right decision the obvious must be stated. When you are really attached to someone the mind has a way of making excuses to justify staying with them, even if the situation is hell. Always look for the bottom line and ask yourself how is this person impacting me? Is it for better or worse? The old saying I can do bad by myself is all too for real in this case.

The Withdrawal

If you come to the conclusion that you are better off without someone, depending on the level of attachment, you should expect some withdrawals. Maybe this person was great at sex – and I'd be the first to admit... this is a very, very real thing. Or maybe it was something else that should *not* justify you being with them. If they make you unhappy, sex nor anything else can make it better

50

– I'm sorry to say... but it's true. Furthermore, when people feel lonely they often end up making the decision to go back. Most people who fall victim to loneliness find themselves in a string of relationships and grow accustom to having someone to call their own. Without someone to take up that space they panic and perceive being alone as a personal problem. Unfortunately, their version of a solution is finding someone to fill the gap with the belief that anyone is better than no one. While some folks might choose wisely or just get lucky, many others don't have such luck. And for the sake of not feeling lonely they entertain a new relationship although it will not last for very long. And even when it does last the experience is usually so bad that they secretly wish it was over. And by the time they come out of it they would have wasted their time and the time of the other person – I think anyone would agree that this is just wrong.

The Restart

Letting go of a situation that is not working gives you an opportunity to start fresh. Not saying that you should jump right back into another relationship because maybe it's best that you take some time to yourself. Giving yourself a moment to breath can help you grow individually and will benefit your next relationship. If your problems are only deepening and progress seems out of reach, then holding on is just slow agony. Freedom and happiness comes with a price and if you want it you have to be willing to pay.

Musiq

EXAMPLE: PART 4 (A LOVE DEFERRED)

After a convo between Monica and Brian, Kimberly decides to intervene

(Text between Monica and Kim)

.ıll L&M   **1:43**

Monica: Kim can u come get me please
Kim: Hey, sure what's wrong?
Monica: girl my car broke down
Kim: Awwh!!!
Kim: Poor baby, I'm sorry, where u at now?
Monica: I'm home
Kim: Okay I'm not far at all actually
Monica: K
Monica: thank u so much
Kim: No prob
Kim: So you know i saw your boy the other day
Monica: really, where
Kim: Girl where else, I went the store, saw him in there looking all sad
Kim: So i walked over and said hi
Kim: We started talking a little bit and he told me what happened
Monica: yeah
Monica: so
Kim: Monica
Monica: what
Kim: Now you know i love like my own sister
Kim: But what's going on wit you?
Kim: Why are you treating him like that, I'll even say he one of the good ones
Kim: And you know ain't that many of them out there
Kim: Why you just dumped your entire past on that boy like that, that can't be right
Monica: I know I know
Monica: girl what's wrong with me
Monica: idk wut happend, i just snapped
Monica: it's like sumthin inside just said "get him"
Kim: Wow, okay
Monica: next thing i know im saying all typsa stuff just to get over
Monica: i just got sooo angry!!!

.ıllL&M   1:43   ▯▯▯▯▮

> **Monica: sad part is it wasn't even about him**
> **Monica: i just felt so bad i couldn't control it**
> **Kim: I feel you girl**
> **Kim: Hey, I'm pullin up now**

Kimberly takes Monica's hand and leads her to the sofa.

"Monica, in your defense you've been through some real stuff in your life, and all of that has taken a toll on you. But you're going to have to stop blaming yourself and using what happened in the past as an excuse to keep up this circus act. I've seen you with guy after guy and they all get the same crazy treatment. Whether upfront or later, eventually you let your pain take over and then everything hits the fan. You're going to have to fix YOU before you can ever expect to love and *be* loved the way you want to."

Monica begins to cry as her friend's very direct and honest words sink in. "I know Kim *sniff* you're so right, but it's just so hard to let it all go. It's just so hard to get over all these emotions." Kimberly slides closer to Monica and embraces her tightly with both arms. "I got you girl, we're going to make it through…"

SIX MONTHS LATER …

Monica scrambles through her purse to find her phone as it vibrates and rings repeatedly.

Monica: Hello….Brian….
Brian: yeah, hey, ummm… can we talk later
Monica: yeah, yes, of course, Is everything okay
Brian: look, we just need to talk, I will be there by six
Monica: Oh… Okay…

He hangs up. Monica sits down on the bed with both hands wrapped around her cell phone. Unsure of what to make of Brian's sudden request to talk, her mind begins to wander. Just a couple of months back Monica revealed to Brian her deep dark past of being a stripper while in college, and much wilder days of being a serial dater… and let's just say she overcame a tiny battle with red wine. And to her surprise he accepted her still, and never once passed judgment. However, she was still concerned that he may have changed his mind about her after having more time to think about it. She then begins to wonder whether or not one of his boys knew something about her and shared it with him. Thought after thought came, adding boatloads of panic and worry until Monica could not take it anymore. She then unlocks her phone and presses the call button to redial the last number on her call list. "Great! The damn voicemail…" It wasn't uncommon for Brian's phone to go to voicemail while he was at work. He was a lawyer and while in the courthouse there was very little signal to be had.

"Dang it, he must be in court." Monica paces back and forth as she resumes thinking about what he might want to talk about. When six o'clock rolled around Brian was rolling up. She knew that he would be prompt because he's always on time. When he enters her apartment the door key was not attached to his key ring. Monica's mouth dropped as she observed him placing the lone key upon the counter.

"What are you doing, Brian?"

Brian makes his way over to the couch and sits down.

"Monica, the last eight months have been hectic to say the least. You've accused me repeatedly of stuff that I've NEVER done or would even think of doing. And no matter what I say and how many times you say you get it and claim to understand, we end up right back where we started. I can't do this anymore…"

With her worst fear realized Monica sits motionless and stares into Brian's eyes. She then breaks out into tears and rolls from the couch onto the floor. Brian places his hand on her back – he feels her body jerk with each sob and quickly pulls back to keep himself from becoming emotional.

"I'm sorry, Monica, I'm so sorry to hurt you. But I just see no reason to continue… " Monica does not respond. Brian stands to his feet and heads for the door. Pausing in the open of the doorway he glances back one final time and just like that he's out of her life.

CHAPTER

142...I LOVE ME

LOVE THY SELF: 'cause if you don't....

Loving yourself is not a selfish thing... well technically it is... but in the best way, and that's a good thing... in fact, it's vitally necessary before you can truly give and receive love in a relationship. It allows you to be with someone without all the crazy hang-ups. Hang-ups are the responses to your own issues with things like an overwhelming feeling of emptiness, a constant battle with insecurities, low self-esteem and so on. You basically end up with internal bruises that in turn require comfort, and when you don't get that comfort you act out in one way or another. When there is a lack of self love poor decisions are often made when it comes to relationships. You might find yourself in a situation that never should have been, or on the flipside only end up chasing off the perfect person because of your problems. Earlier in the book I mentioned the importance of completing your individual journey before joining it with another person. If you still have a ways to travel on your personal walk... then keeping up with someone else won't be easy. What then happens is that you are forced to abandon your own walk, naturally, because you are no longer doing it alone. And because you are now giving to someone else what you once gave only to yourself, the emptiness is automatically directed toward your relationship. And if not handled correctly it can become very destructive. When there is emptiness it is impossible for a man or woman to fix it for you. They might be able to temporarily ease the pain through compliments – but no matter how often they tell you that you are beautiful, it will never stick if you don't know it for yourself.

THE EMPTINESS: Look Out... It's A Trap!

People not loving themselves is something both men and women struggle with. However, women are hit the hardest by this trap. And fellas, this is not to say that you are off the hook, but I want to really connect with the ladies through this message. Let me start by saying that men are a big part of why women are more susceptible to this trap... and here's what I mean. If you turn on your television, radio, or open up a magazine, in one way or another women are told what they should look like to be accepted. Men, too, find themselves under the gun of a certain image portrayed in the media – but I think we can all agree that it's not that deep compared to that of women. Over the years through relationships, friends, family, and traveling... I have seen a good amount of women... good women, beautiful, awesome and amazing women, fall into these traps. I could go on for days but for your sake and mine I won't bore you with it – but I do want to touch on a few points. My goal is to help the ladies avoid these traps, and also encourage the fellas to be more sensitive and to make yourself aware of how you might be adding to the problem. And for the many men who are trapped themselves don't worry, I didn't forget about you.

YOU LOVING YOU: If You don't... who will?!?

Loving yourself is more than just saying it or taking yourself to the mall. We see this very common and alluring mistake every day – people out trying to buy their happiness with things to cover up what they've been taught not to love. In my examples, Monica is one of those people – always looking for something to help her feel better about herself according to what society, the media, and a hard life has dealt her. In order for most things to work right, like self love, your foundation has to be in place. Otherwise you will spend your entire life trying to make up for a cracked base that is constantly shifting and breaking away. Ask yourself what are the things that you do to make up for a messed up foundation. Is it shopping, sex, relationships, money, or what? When you find yourself constantly chasing these things and never satisfied, that's just your emptiness looking for comfort. You're hurting on the inside and the runaway train of emotions will only build in momentum overtime. You don't have to wait for it to crash, you can do something about it right here and right now.

Maybe you feel that you are overweight or too skinny... or how about you want more muscles or to be taller. We all struggle with something either past or current, and no one should be judged or made to feel bad about their insecurities, however, in order to give more in a relationship you have to deal with or at least gain some control over your issues. And when working to overcome

59

these shortcomings you have to be honest with yourself. For instance, if you are overweight, and are sensitive to gestures or comments made toward overweight individuals, you have two ways to look at it... 1: you being overweight just might've needed someone to shed light on the situation because your health could be at risk, or simply 2: to motivate you to change your physical appearance to your liking and doing something about it. If the issue is more social and unrelated to health... like say you dislike your skin color or some other purely socially conflicting thing – then you might want to find a good book on that topic and really apply the lessons to your life. There are countless reasons that might cause a person to lack love for themselves, but we don't have to make a point of all of them. Bottom line, until you are able to look inside and face whatever it is that makes you *YOU,* you cannot even begin to deal with the problem. When you love yourself, and I'm saying truly love yourself, there will be no more chasing relationships for the wrong reasons. You can then be with someone fully, WITHOUT the strain of emptiness pulling at you. And although one problem or another might find its way into your relationship, they will not control the tone or pace of it. So don't be disappointed when the occasional problem arises – just acknowledge it, accept it, do what you can to make it better, and move on... there's way too much joy in love to waste time and energy on things that are painful. So please, do yourself a huge favor and LOVE YOURSELF!!!

EXAMPLE: PART 5 (RELEASE... RESET... RESTART)

The next day following the breakup with Brian, Monica tries her best to keep her mind off of it while at work. But regardless of her attempts at keeping the pain at bay the thoughts begin creeping in one by one. Blaming herself... blaming him... wondering why no one wants to love her... blaming her past and anything else that might explain her love life misfortunes. By early afternoon Monica's emotions had boiled over. To keep everyone at work from seeing her breakdown she quickly leaves her desk and heads for the exit. When she reaches the front door she notices her boss and a few others out front talking. She turns around and heads for the break room in hopes of finding some solitude there. When she reaches the break room there was only one person who luckily was finishing up their lunch and heading back out. Not wanting her coworkers to see her in tears she rushes into a closet located in the corner of the break room. As she enters the closet, the wet floor sign hanging from the door is flung from its hook from the force of her opening the door and entering the darkened 6x8 room. Lost in her emotions and a river of tears Monica had not realized that the sign had fallen off. Moments later she hears footsteps enter the break room. Whoever it was they seemed to be headed toward the sink. Suddenly the footsteps stop, when they continued the steps were now headed in Monica's direction. They were now right outside of the closet door and Monica watches as the shadow curves over to pick up the wet floor sign. Then the knob turns and the closet door slowly opens.

"Monica?" Her boss says with uncertainty as she peers further into the darkened closet to make sure it was her.

"Yeah Stacey, it's me. I'm so sorry, I'm just having a moment right now..." Stacey enters the closet and kneels down next to her.

"Get up sweetheart, I think it's time that we talk. I want you to take the rest of the day off and tomorrow after work I would like to have a one on one session with you." Monica tries to gather herself as she struggles a bit while making her way through the break room to the doorway. She finally gets to her car, drives off, and goes home. The next day after work Stacey locks the door as the last employee makes their exit. Before returning to her office where Monica waited she noticed a familiar car pull into the parking lot. It was her cousin, Michael, who had left her a message not too long ago about needing to talk to her. She had been so busy that she forgot to return his call. She unlocks the door and opens it up.

"Michael, hi, I'm so sorry I never got back to you, I've just been so darn busy…"

"It's okay cuz… I know you have a lot going on in your world, so I decided to just come by and see if I could catch you at your office."

"Well, you found me, come on in."

Michael rolls up his window and parks his car near the front door of the office. He jumps out and walks up and hugs Stacey. He then enters and she closes the door and locks it behind him. Already familiar with the layout of her building, Michael immediately heads back to her office. Stacey remembers that Monica is waiting there as well but by then it's too late. She walks quickly to catch up with Michael, but by the time she makes it to her office they're already carrying on a conversation. Stacey politely interrupts and apologizes to Monica before introducing Michael as her cousin. She then tells Michael that her and Monica are about to talk one on one for an hour or two and gave him the option to wait in the lobby. Michael glances back over to Monica and smiles followed by an apology. He grabs his jacket and heads for the lobby. Although Monica had no idea what he was there for, she could tell that he too needed Stacey. She thought to herself that possibly he was having similar problems. Just as he makes it into the hallway Monica calls out and invites him to stay. She assures Stacey that she doesn't mind. Surprised, Michael raises both eyebrows and looks back over at Monica as if to see whether or not she meant what she said. Sensing that Monica was sincere, Michael quickly turns to Stacey for her approval and receives a head nod followed by a smile. Michael sits down and the conversation begins.

Love According to Musiq

ACT II

LOVING YOU

Act II is all about loving another person through understanding and accepting who they are. With loving yourself out of the way... I want you to turn your attention to that "special someone" and what it means to let them in fully. You cannot let anyone all the way in when you're fighting to accept who they are. Learn to love through embracing the differences of others, no matter their gender, culture, style, and so on...

CHAPTER

SEX

The way SHE thinks it···and HE sees it

I doubt that a woman will ever fully grasp a man's perspective on sex. On the same token, I also think that men have a lot to learn about the sexual thinking of women. When it comes to the act of sex for most men... more often than not... it's just that... sex! Almost like going out to grab some food or having a drink. The need comes and is taken care of, and pretty much... that's it. Not to be crass about it, I'm just stating the facts. Now, in a relationship scenario, sex for men does become something more as it takes on a deeper meaning. Although a man's underlying feeling about sex doesn't change, there is a shift in how he views the act and goes about it when it comes to you. As the woman he loves, your feelings now matter on a much deeper level, or in other words... it becomes something way more than just a squirrel out to get a nut... so to speak. He now sees you as his woman, a lady, someone who deserves a specific level of admiration – and with it comes the responsibility of both pleasing and respecting you. For you women, however, being in an exclusive relationship offers an opportunity to let go and feed your sexual appetite as often as you want without the concern of being labeled a hoe or worse. Of course I know there are some who could give a damn about the opinions of others and society and just do them. And for the record let me say that women desire sex just as much as men – and in some cases more. The difference is how we go about it. The male libido on average is higher than that of a woman's mostly because of how we've been conditioned to respond to sex. Factors like "hoe" or "slut" and other pressures are put on women as early as childhood. I mean, what woman is okay with being a hoe? Is that not a strike against what being a "lady" is all about? Boys on the other hand are encouraged to hunt and are often measured by the successes of their hunts. Many mothers of young boys are also guilty of contributing to this type of gender molding... And I promise my intention is not to judge, not even in the absolute least... so please bear with me on this for a minute and just think about it – but how many times have you heard a mom talk about her handsome son being a heartbreaker when he grows up? What do you think that is? It sure as heck isn't the same way daughters are treated.   By the time adulthood rolls around you have two sets of people with God given sex drives, however, one is told to suppress it while the other is encouraged to act on it. So when the time comes to "hook up" there's going to be an inevitable clash of wills – and we wonder why men and women are mostly on different pages when it comes to sex.

Battle of the Sexes: It Ain't Just Is What It Is

Society alone is not responsible for our differences. I mean, a man by nature will feel the need to "hit–it" when an attractive female falls in his path. There is nothing at all wrong with this urge, it's very normal actually, but it can cause problems as we all know. If a woman feels that her virtues are not being honored and respected, she's more likely than not going to push back. Of course this depends on the situation, because maybe at that moment she couldn't care less about virtues... of which I am neither condemning nor condoning. To better understand and deal with the differences between men and women when it comes to sex – we have to be more considerate of one another. Ladies, you should know from the gate that a man wants to get you in bed, no matter what he says or does, no matter how passive or aggressive he goes about it. And don't get me wrong, he may very well be a nice and sweet guy with all the right intentions... but just know that without a doubt **heeee's thinking about it**. Furthermore, women are usually thinking the same thing in the beginning but somehow forget this while upholding their "virtues". I just don't think there's anything wrong with wanting to act on the sexual feelings you may have for the person you're attracted to, as long as you are clear and certain about where each other stands when it comes down to it. As a rule of thumb, men should keep in mind that sex isn't *just* sex for most women – and when you forget this reality you will wish you would had remembered, one way or another. And the sooner women accept the fact that the average man is *mostly* driven by sex when entertaining a woman he's into, the better off they will be. I mean look ladies... why in the world would you stress over something that you can do nothing about... especially when it's something that you want and expect in a relationship yourself.

What Men Do For Sex: ...anything

The way society dictates sexual behavior has its ups and downs. I doubt a society flooded with women who pursued sex like men would be much of a society at all. And although I am not complaining about this balance, it does create an environment where a lot of men turn to deceit in order to get their sexual fill. A lot of women are surprised when a man pulls a disappearing act after they have sex... when obviously that's all he wanted from the start! This is nothing new, and as long as men are able to run game they will. And although it's never cool to mislead anyone, women should come to grips with this reality, and if it happens learn from it and move on. I can't think of anything worse for a woman than trying to keep alive something that never was. I would never encourage any woman to sleep around, there are just way too many problems and labels that come with it – *however*, getting sex out of the way, sooner than later, can become quite useful when it comes to finding out what a man is really about. For most men when it comes to wanting a woman, they will say just about anything short of "kill me" to get at her – and however you go about seeing through a man's motives, just remember that the whole truth will only come out *after* sex. Until this happens you are not really dealing with "*the man*", but rather a man in pursuit of your goods. This is where knowing what you're looking for comes in handy. When you know where you want to be you can ask the right questions and set the proper tone to reduce or even flat out avoid men who aren't about anything. With standards comes a high wall that most men with the wrong intentions will not attempt to climb. Men who are out for the goods only are looking for easy prey, but with standards the easy stamp is wiped from your forehead. Chasing sex can be very expensive and time consuming, especially when there's multiple women involved. A good challenge, *aka "standards"*, will keep the wrong men at bay... and it just might be enough to convince him to do the right thing. Consider this; people who avoid commitment were more than likely hurt in the past or simply misdirected. The past has a way of making life hell for the present, and that is why a person must always start with themselves. And with yourself set straight you might, *just might*, be able to help someone else get straight, too – but that's totally up to you.

EXAMPLE: PART 6 (WHEN TO HOLD'EM... WHEN TO FOLD'EM)

The smell of coffee was thick in the air as Stacey passed both Michael and Monica fresh cups. Monica goes first and begins with a question concerning men and sex.

"What's up with men and sex? It's like they're down for just about anything just to get some, even if it destroys someone's life – and then wonder why most women are slow to give it up." Stacey smiles in response, Monica continues. "It almost kinda makes a sistah wanna just be a nun..." Michael remains silent but follows her every word with great interest. Stacey holds her words until she is sure that Monica has finished.

"Well Monica, I hear what you are saying and you have a valid point. There is a problem with a lot of men who are out for just one thing. But what you should remember is that their motives and actions don't have to become your problems. And these things become your problem when you are unrealistic about them. Yes, men think about sex from the time they wake up to the moment they go to sleep, and even then you can bet just about anything that they're dreaming about it! But the more interesting thing about this is that in our own way as women, so do we. This is a very natural part of us, and by no means should be viewed as bad. The problem comes in

72

when sex is used as a tool to get and keep a man. Girl let me tell you something, you will never really know what a man wants until after you give him some... 'cause right when it's over, his little man is doing less of the thinking and the big head resumes command. Now, I'm not saying that *men* don't know what they want before sex – *what* I'm saying is *you* won't know what they want." Monica's eyes widen as she takes in the information.

"Well, honestly Stacey I would rather *not* give up the goods just to see whether or not he's sincere about being in a relationship. I mean, *been there done that* and that 'doesn't' even begin to cover it, and I don't want to walk that path anymore."

"Look... I hear you and I feel your pain, and please don't mistake what I'm saying, I'm only making a point to point out something that all of us ladies know, whether through the grape vine or experience – and that is that once you give a man some who's not about anything, he won't hang around for much longer – and if he does you will notice a change in his attitude." Monica nods her head in agreement and thinks back on the many times that it's happened to her. Stacey watches her reaction and continues. "At the end of the day, there's not really much you can do about the things men would do for sex. However, if your standards are intact the way you carry yourself will make a *no-good* man think three times before trying you."

73

CHAPTER

MONEY

What it means to Him and does for Her

A Man & His Money

Like sex... money has its place in our society when it comes to relationships. As boys we men learn to associate attracting women with several things; like for example physical attributes, material possessions, words, and yes.....money. Women are also provided some direction when it comes to attracting the opposite sex. But we will discuss that later because for them money is rarely a tool used to get a man because they don't need it. For most men, a woman's goods are worth a million bucks....literally. Of the many ways men are taught to get a woman, it's no surprise that money is among the top. It's just that simple and we all know that a large portion of men associate themselves with their wallet. The reality is that we understand the power behind being able to provide for the ones we love and care for... or in this case... buy the things women like. And at the end of the day the more money we have the more confident we are when it comes to women. Although most men seem to accept this, there are some who like to play dumb and not give credit where credit is due. Bottom line, females drive the world and that's why us men have to push so damn hard! A man and his money work together like partners when after a woman. Because women feel appreciated and generally tend to gravitate toward nice gifts and so on – our response as men is to "GO GET" those things, and that could mean long hours, back breaking work in the sun, overtime, different hustles, credit cards, you name it. Have a man's credit all jacked up just on

Musiq

the strength of that walk... damn! And it doesn't matter how virtuous or classy a woman might consider herself to be, a man has to show some degree of success or potential in order for her to take that step. And no I am not talking about a one night stand. When I say that step I mean a real relationship. And for you fellas who see these women as goal diggers, you obviously don't understand nor appreciate the reality of the situation... no woman wants a loser. And being a loser is not about whether you are balling or not, but instead your outlook on life and how you go about living it. A real woman, depending on where she is in life, doesn't require a man to be exactly where he aims to be. But he should at least know where the hell he's going. We're talking about someone who might father your children someday, and that family will depend on him for support in more ways than just money. If your head is not in the right place then I'm sorry dude... that's a problem. Being clear about what genuine expectations are versus gold digging is something guys should understand before calling a woman with standards such a degrading term. Now, if you ARE a gold digger then don't be runnin' game trying to disguise your vindictive intentions as standards. Keep it real and play your part and don't mess it up for the ladies who are actually about something! *Ooh I really wanna use a word so bad right now*... but out of the love and respect I have for the many *women* reading this (thank u btw) I'm gonna choose not to... but I know *you* know what I mean!

Check!?!

Sharing is caring… I know… I get that, I really do… however, when it comes to men and women, I don't agree that us men HAVE to pick up the check every time we go out. I know some of you might say "*that's just the way it is…*" am I right? But who makes those rules anyway? I think that you should do what works for you and yours and not what somebody else thinks is best. Yes, we men want to pay and don't mind paying… when we can. This is another way of saying "I can take care of my woman". What do you think we work so hard for? Now on the other hand, a man wants to know that his woman has his back as well. Maybe his money is a little off at the moment, and he needs for you to pick up the slack. There's nothing like a woman stepping up to the plate and whipping out her purse to cover the check from time to time. Also ladies it wouldn't hurt to step up and pay even if he has the money to cover everything. This is an opportunity to strengthen the bond between you and your man. He might act all tough and push back and tell you that he wants to pay, of which I'm sure he means, but inside he's saluting you. Us guys are simple and those kinds of gestures go a long *looong* way. Now if your man tries to turn this into an everyday thing knowing good and well he can pay, then he's just being cheap at that point. However you decide to work it out in your relationship is up to you – just don't fall into a pattern of scheduling turns of who pays for what. Doing that is just overkill and will create problems for you. Eventually someone is going to get mad because they had to pay for the last five outings... according to the tab. Taking care of each other should just happen. And when it comes to paying, a man should be honest with himself and his lady about his ability to afford certain things – it's also important for women to be considerate when it comes to spending. Knowing that for the most part men will go out of their way to show their lady a good time, it's only right not to take advantage of that. You don't have to *ballout* every time you step out. A little compromise here and there shows support and puts a man at ease. Otherwise over time he will become stressed about his woman's picky nature and his inability to completely satisfy her regardless of how much he spends. A man never wants to feel as if he cannot adequately provide for you. He might as well just come out and say "baby....I can't take care of you". Whether or not you get why men think this way doesn't change the fact that we do. Even if your man makes very good money it never hurts to show some consideration by being a little more economical from time to time.

The Female Breadwinner

First let me get one thing out the way... a man who feels threatened by a woman who makes more money has the wrong idea about what it means to be in a relationship... in my opinion. If your woman is making more money than you then that's more money for the pot! So the whole emasculation of a man by his woman being more financially stable is irrelevant. GET OVER YOURSELF BRO! But now ladies, just because you make more money doesn't mean that you have the right to give any less respect to the man in your life. And the same thing goes for the fellas, too. The money you make should have nothing at all to do with the love you give or the respect you show. If someone is only good enough to be respected when their money is good, then it's not them you respect but their bank status. As far as women are concerned, there is a growing trend of breadwinners that I don't see stopping anytime soon. More women are earning college degrees and not to mention they represent a quickly rising number in the workforce. There are a lot of men who are seriously threatened by this. They feel that somehow women will no longer need them. This could not be further from the truth. The only thing a woman doesn't need is a man with little confidence. Just like we need support to do bigger and better things, women do as well. And never should a woman be made to feel guilty about going after her goals. Fellas... in order to get respect we have to give it and your woman doing big things is no exception. As the value of a person's net worth goes up, the value of everyday gestures should not go down. Some people have the tendency to become a little uppity when their money grows, losing appreciation for the smaller things. Whether or not you are into high fashion or candy bars, if your man or woman goes out of their way to buy something for you, the intention behind it should come before the price tag. No matter who brings home the most money there should never be a loss of respect. Making little side comments to rub it in someone's face is just unnecessary. If the happiness of your relationship has a dollar value, then you've got a lot more than just money to worry about. There's nothing wrong with making money, just don't let the money make you do dumb things, like putting it before those you claim to love... and that's real.

EXAMPLE: PART 7 (SCARRED MONEY)

Moving on with the conversation Michael brings up the issue of women and money and how it has affected his relationships. He expresses to Stacey that just about every woman that he's dated has been more into his money than him. Looking for guidance he asks Stacey to explain what he might be doing wrong.

"Well Michael, as your cousin, your close cousin at that, I am very familiar with your personality. And I've also had the opportunity to observe how you interact with some of your female companions. By losing your father at such a young age and not having him around could possibly play into your lack of self confidence. Although you are a very intelligent man and great at what you do, you lack a tremendous amount of confidence in your personal life, and women can sniff that right out. Unfortunately, the type of women who generally pursue you are cash predators. They see you with this great job and plenty of money, and not to mention passive – so it's kind of like a pay day when they lay eyes on you. And while these women are in fact wrong for pursuing you in this manner... YOU are responsible for who you allow into your life." With both hands resting in his lap and all ten fingers interlocked, Michael lowers his head and stares into his open palms. Without lifting his head he turns his neck toward Monica and gestures as if to say "She's good..."

Musiq

Monica chimes in and brings up another point dealing with men who feel insecure about women who make more money than they do. Stacey laughs before taking a sip of her coffee. "Oh yeah, this is definitely a problem. I am all too familiar with men who think they are too good to make less." Monica readjusts herself in anticipation for the rest of Stacey's reply. "Sometimes when men feel this way, I will agree to some justification, but there are other times I simply cannot. And by justification, I'm not suggesting that it's ever okay to be jealous of a woman or man for making more money, but I've seen situations where women will throw it in a man's face, in one way or another, about the fact that she makes the most money. Whether or not she does this directly or indirectly... either way it's wrong. No one, man or woman, should ever be made to feel that they're a non factor simply because they bring in less money, this is nonsense and egotistical at best. If a woman cannot appreciate her man outside of how much money he makes, then she just doesn't need to be with him. On the other hand, if a man cannot accept the fact that his woman makes more money, then the same goes for him.

CHAPTER

FRIENDS & FAMILY

When Outside influences become Inside Distractions

Musiq

Friends: Who's really who

There's nothing like a good friend who has your back. Someone who gives you advice and supports you through thick and then. I can personally speak to this and know that good friendships are invaluable in life. The other side of friendship has a slightly different spin to it. This is where boundaries are crossed and the once supportive homie becomes judge and jury over your other relationships. A good friend can be very helpful when it comes to listening to your problems and helping you work through stuff, but for a lot of men and women the all too faithful friend can sometimes create more problems than solutions. In a relationship between a man and a woman, a friend's place is never to call the shots. If your decisions are made after consulting your so-called friend then chances are you're not doing what's best for your own sake or your relationship. I'm not trying to paint a picture that having friends weigh in on certain decisions is wrong because that just isn't true. Friends can remind us of where we come from without worrying about being dumped. Sometimes the ugly truth is what we need to keep us in check, and only a true friend can be respected for being honest and standing up for what they truly feel is right with your best interest at heart. So when it comes to friendships, I strongly encourage that you nurture and appreciate them. And if you want to get technical about it, we know that a good friendship can benefit a person's overall health and quality of life.   What you should aim for is balance, regardless whether it's a friend or significant other. Your friends have their place, which is not the same as that special someone. When lines get crossed that's when problems are created. So do yourself and your relationships a favor and keep the situation balanced.

The Parent Trap: Daddy's Girl... Momma's Boy

Anyone who's with or has been with a person whose parents are all in the mix knows how frustrating it can be. You want to ask them; "who are you with, me or your parents?". But of course if you go there you run the risk of creating more problems. So in this case what can you do?   Well... until that person decides to detach themselves from the "parental hip" there's really nothing much that can be done.   On the other hand it doesn't necessarily mean trouble just because a parent is involved in their adult child's life. The problem is when the parents can't seem to distinguish between their relationship with their son or daughter versus the one that *you* have with them.   Naturally this can cause friction in a relationship, especially when your man or woman gives in to the pull of their parents instead of standing up for what they really want.   And let's not MISTAKE standing your ground with being disrespectful. Of course respect is very important when it comes to parents. But the same thing goes for you and your situation, and as an adult your parents should respect your decisions and not demand that you live according to their wants. If you find yourself in a situation that is dangerous and draws the attention of people on the outside, then that's something different. You should appreciate a sincere attempt to rectify the situation from someone who's only out to help. However, there's a huge difference between that and a parent trying to control your life. In a relationship, having respect for the other person can be demonstrated in several ways. And how you manage outside relationships is a big part of that respect. Not to say that friends and family are not important, but how can you expect to truly be happy if you are always held hostage to someone else's likes and dislikes. Sounds to me like a crazy way to live. Give that special someone a chance to make you happy, and just so long as you aren't being abused or abusive, then I don't think there's anything wrong with putting your interests first – otherwise you may never find happiness for yourself.

When it comes to parents dictating to grown children how to live, you ladies get it the worst. There is nothing like a dad who believes that no one is good enough for his little girl. What ends up happening is either a totally unhappy father or a completely unhappy daughter. This is because either A: the dad gets what he wants; or B: the daughter does. Sometimes it works out in everyone's favor, like say when the overzealous father hits it off really well with his daughter's man of choice. And for all you momma's boys out there, it's so vitally important that you make room for the "new" mama in your life. You have to stand up and set things straight by not taking either side, but assuring both sides that they have a special place in your heart. And I'm not saying that just any man or woman should be given this type of consideration with family and friends. In the end it's more about the principle of getting the people you care about to respect your personal life… PERIOD. This will kill any drama that would otherwise be created.

Everyone else

We've all been guilty of it at one time or another. Letting outside influences dictate to us who we appreciate and why. I've personally dated women who I felt were downright beautiful… perfect just the way they were… but let them tell it they were pretty much the worst thing walking around. You don't have to be skinny, or thick for that matter, to be sexy or beautiful. The world is full of all kinds of opinions that people recycle and keep alive, and it's up to you to step out of the way of whatever doesn't pertain to you. It makes no sense to me for reused opinions to control how you feel about yourself and other people. And if you have somebody in your life… or when you find that someone… be sure to let them know how beautiful they are to you – because the world won't hesitate to tell them otherwise.

EXAMPLE: 8 (LOOKIN' FOR MOM IN ALL THE WRONG PLACES)

Stacey talks to Michael about listening to his mother too much and going off of his own gut. Michael gets a phone call and it's his mom. He steps outside for a few minutes to talk. When he returns she asks how she's doing, Michael states she's fine and makes a comment under his breath that he wishes more women were like his mother. Stacey hears him and immediately dives in.

"So Michael, do you look for the women you date to be more like your mother?"

"Well, no, not really... Although I do wish that more women were as consistent as her when it comes to their attitude, and not to mention cooking and cleaning, and so on."

"So it sounds to me that you're comparing the women you date to your mother?"

"Well, I don't try to... but I guess it does kind of happen."

"Well first let me say this... as long as you're going around looking for women to be like your mother, you will never find true happiness. The kind of happiness that a wife or girlfriend brings to a man's life has nothing to do with your mother and shouldn't be compared. My advice to you is to find out who you truly are, embrace it, and allow the confidence that I know you have to shine through and STOP looking for your "mom" in these women, because you already have one. What you need now is a lover, and it isn't fair to critique them according to the impossible task of being your mother."

Stacey's phone rings and she asks them to excuse her for just a few minutes. While Stacey is on the phone, Michael and Monica continue talking. Monica asks Michael if he has any children and he tells her no. Monica then goes into her purse and pulls out a picture of her princess and hands it to Michael. Michael smiles and admits that he loves children and compliments her on a beautiful daughter. Just then Stacey hangs up the phone and asks to see the picture. Although she had met Monica's daughter several times before, she hadn't seen this particular photo. She smiles and passes the 4x6 photo back to Monica. Noticing the chemistry between the two, Stacey decides to talk about kids and how they fit into new relationships.

CHAPTER

WHEN KIDS "R" INVOLVED

The Reality, The Risks, & The Rules

What About The Children?

When kids are added to the mix a whole new dimension is created and their safety is a parent's priority. If you're one of those parents who don't feel this way then after you finish with this book you should read up on "good" parenting... no, seriously. As a father my son is

!!! EVERTHING !!!

to me, and his needs are my responsibility. So for all of you single parents out there I stand with you. I want to also connect with those of you who may have inherited a family through marriage or even from dating someone who already has kids. Whatever the case there are three main things I'd like for you to consider:

• The Reality: The truth, the whole truth, and nothing but the truth

• The Risks: What parents must factor in and what step-parents must consider

• The Rules: Your role, his/her role, and of course... the children's role

Whether you like it or not things change when kids enter the picture. There are more people to consider on either side than just the two of you. When folks start forgetting stuff and doing their own thing, you can bet there will be problems. If you want to grow as a couple, whether you or the other person has kids, then you must learn to live by the rules.

The Reality: For the Children

The truth of the matter is that when there's an addition to your life (*children*) the duties that come with it don't change no matter who comes or goes. A child's needs should remain a top priority, and your responsibility to meet those needs should as well. Of course if you're one of those "other kinds" of parents, then I'll leave that one for you and DFACS. Now, for those of us who give a damn about our offspring and want to do our best as parents *and* lovers and not one or the other, the very first thing that must be done is accepting the reality of the situation. It's never a good idea to be with someone who does not like your kids or kids in general. You probably won't know at first whether or not your child is liked or not, but in due time it will more than likely show. If the person you meet does not have kids of their own then it won't be easy to know what they are like as parents. If they have nieces, nephews, or a child in their life who they are close to, then that may give you a little taste of their parenting ability.

The Risks: For Parents

If you have children then you know that with youngsters comes a whole new level of commitment. Being responsible for every aspect of their life is a task that many people quickly run away from. And when you bring someone new into your life, and there are children involved, they also have to consider the situation as a potential step parent. Not to mention the time split between the children and the other person. For those of you who don't have children and currently with or just met someone who does, be sure not to judge or assume the worst. Not to downplay the situation... but sometimes becoming a single parent just happens, whether by divorce or otherwise – and with the many possibilities of someone becoming a single parent, the odds of you finding and falling in love with one are high. The question now becomes, are you ready to accept the reality of this type of situation if you find yourself in it? The risks come without saying and sometimes without warning. This is why it is so important to choose wisely. Not that you can read through a person and see where their mind is at, but the more mentally and emotionally stable you are, the better off you will be in your selection process. And I hate to make it sound all technical by calling it a "selection process", but in most ways... that's pretty much what it is, and it's a very important process if what you're looking for is long-term. You should always think of the kids when looking for that special someone. The last thing you want to do is bring a crazy person around. That's never good for anyone, parents or children.

The Rules: For Everyone

Now I want you to keep in mind that the "Rules" for your situation may be nothing like that of another's. If nothing else, I am hoping that you take away from this portion the need to acknowledge a situation for what it is, and put the necessary provisions in place to create the best environment for you, them, and the kids.

-Your role

As a parent, as I'm sure you know, being in a relationship with kids is something like a juggling act. You want to give the kids enough time, affection, attention, and support to make sure they grow with a healthy amount of confidence and love in their heart. I think we all know what can happen if a child is neglected by their parents – grades suffer, behavior suffers, and then of course life overall becomes a nightmare in many ways. So let's say you've decided to bring someone special into your life, without question a little math is required because your time will inevitably be divided. Not to go backwards... but by this time you should have considered, to the best of your ability, who this person is that you've chosen to bring into the fold. Although most people will not show you who they really are upfront, some tell tale signs here and there should be noted when getting to know someone. And this should be the case whether you have kids or not. Now, back to the kid part. I am more than likely right that most sensible parents are not into rushing things when it comes to someone new meeting their kids. You probably have a list of your own reasons in addition to the obvious ones why you should take it slow... but I would like to take this opportunity to mention a couple:

Kids have a tendency of growing attached, especially when they really like someone... also, what if it doesn't work out? A child seeing mom or dad in and out of relationships is probably not the best way to set an example for them. So maybe before an introduction ever takes place, it would be a good idea to give that person a briefing of what they're getting themselves into. Maybe your kids, or kid, are bad as hell and you want to brace the other person for what they are getting involved with – something like how soldiers in war are briefed before going on a mission – oh... *I'm sorry, I know, all children are perfect little angels... so I apologize* – aaahhh stop acting like you don't know what I'm talking about! I'm just sayin', this way when that special someone meets your "less than orderly" kids, they won't be like "what the hell?!". Give the newcomer a chance to mentally adjust and ready themselves, so whenever the meeting does take place, the building can begin immediately because there is already some knowledge of the kids, and you never know – the kids may have a lot in common with your new man or woman.

And on the flipside, this same principle is good for the kids as well. When the time is right, sit them down and ask what they think about mom or dad dating someone new. Get their opinions, answers, or whatever questions they may have. If you have kids or have been around someone with kids in this type of situation, you know that they can be quite protective when it comes to their parents. And this is a good sign when you think about it. Better than them growing used to new people and seeing it as normal. A parent is like a mediator in this situation... They are responsible, and should want to be, for making sure things flow smoothly. After the introduction is made, you may want to keep an eye on the development of this extra relationship. Watch how the kids respond to them, and vice versa. The best feedback you could possibly receive would be from the kids themselves. Especially if they are really young – because we all know how they can be, kids don't care, they'll keep it straight up, raw and all the way real!

-Their role

For those of you coming into or are currently involved in a situation with children that are not biologically yours, you do have your part, which is a very important one. As the other adult in the situation your response to the kids matters too, because you are stepping in as a parent, role model, and whatever else serves the needs of the situation. Being ready for resistance when it comes to the children cannot be overstressed. Although not every child will make trouble for someone new in their parent's life, there are some who simply loath the thought of mom or dad being with somebody *other* than the biological parent. And never should this be taken personal or even more importantly...

taken out on the kids. They will come around but only if you show them respect by acknowledging the way they feel. Maybe their parents got a divorce and they are suffering emotionally over it. You are a part of the healing process whether you like it or not. Sometimes all a child needs to hear is that you acknowledge the role of the other parent and you are not trying to make them irrelevant in any way. If you do NOT like kids, and I'm not judging you if you don't, then you should think about that before getting involved with someone who does – **DON'T BE SELFSH!!!** A parent, a *good one that is*, is going to *make* time for their child, as they should. It's wrong to take away from what the kids receive because you want this person all to yourself. Instead, how about you consider some ways to contribute by helping out with homework, pick-ups and drop-offs, running errands if ever necessary, or simply being supportive. Bottom line, if you do not possess the capacity to care for his or her child/children as though they were your own, then your relationship with the parent will never reach its full potential.

-The kids' role

If you're wondering what role a kid could possibly have in this... just read on. A kid's role is basically the parent's instructions. The only way that the situation will ever work is if there is respect from all corners of the relationship, and that includes the kids. Teaching your kids to respect adults goes for personal relationships too, not just teachers and elders. Any parent will tell you that there

Musiq

are exceptions to every rule, and by that I mean a child should respect adults, however... all that goes out the window if it isn't returned. Your instructions should include coming to you ASAP... if ANYONE, and please I do mean ANYONE, steps over the line in ANY way, or even attempts to. I know that every situation may be different, and what might work for me may not work for you, but that's okay because the relative truth behind having a relationship with kids involved is the same for everyone – and this truth is that respect can only come through the acceptance of the situation. And in order to fully accept the situation, everyone must know what they are getting themselves into and that's where communication from the start comes into play. You can't just hope things are going to go the way you want them to – and if that's how you choose to go about it then you are asking for trouble... or you don't really plan to be in the relationship for too long. Do what's best for yourself and your relationship, but most of all for the kids!

EXAMPLE: PART 9 (THERE'S A YOUNG WORLD AFTER ALL)

Stacey takes a sip of her coffee and turns her attention to Monica to address her love life and her daughter...

"There are three things that everyone should consider when getting into a relationship where kids are involved: The Reality, the Risks, and the Rules. The reality is that the relationship will naturally be impacted with youngsters running around. As a parent, a good one that is, you should beware of people who don't like kids, or at least lacks the ability to learn to love yours as their own. This is important because you could marry this person and you want to make sure that they have your child's best interest at heart and nothing less. Do your children a favor and make sure that they are safe until you know for sure who you are dealing with. And even after you know that they are safe, you never stop making sure that they stay safe. And this doesn't mean making the other person feel uncomfortable, but rather communicating with your kids and not ignoring signs that might indicate a problem. The last one is Rules, and this goes for both the 'newcomer' and the 'children'. Just as much as the new man or woman in your life should respect the kiddies, the kiddies should respect them. A positive stepparent relationship is not

Musiq

possible if the kids are not held to any sort of accountability when it comes to the new person. If the position you hold in a child's parent's life impacts them significantly and directly,

then like it or not you have some skin in the game. Therefore how you choose to conduct yourself when in their presence matters, as well as interactions with the parent, and especially with them!"

ACT III

LOVING US

With both sides at peace with themselves and the reality of
who their partner is, a true love relationship is now
possible. Act III is the result of Act I and Act II combined,
and what a true understanding on both sides can create.

CHAPTER

THE TYPE pt.1

Wife Material

We have all probably sat back, male or female, and listened to that woman who knew good and well she had no business talking about becoming somebody's wife. She could have been your friend, your sister, co-worker, or whoever – complaining over why men won't marry her. Seemingly oblivious to the connection between how she carries herself and the men who pass her up when it comes to marriage. Now, in defense of this "hypothetical" woman I just mentioned... she could have had a bad shake at life, but at some point if she wants to find the love she really wants, some changes have to be made, so right now... I want to explain the difference between getting a man and keeping one.

You would think, with the thousands upon thousands of times this topic has been touched on, that "some women" or "those women", whoever you are, would have gotten it right by now. But like most other things with a seemingly easy fix, this topic has deeper roots than you might think. I want to talk about those roots and make some comparisons between what real men appreciate and respond to, compared to what they leave behind. And as for the men, don't worry, I've got you coming next chapter. And speaking of men it's important that you not only look at what *women* are doing, but also yourselves. Without getting too far into the guy part right now I just want to say that there's a huge double standard when it comes to men and women in this case. Unfortunately, though, many women allow the nonsense to continue and even worse, encourage it. We'll get more into all of that later, but first... do me a favor and open up your minds and not only read the material, but prepare to apply it to your life as well. If you believe that you are "IT" when it comes to being a potential wife, I am not here to burst your bubble. I just want to give you an alternative lane of thought to consider outside of your own opinion as it relates to yourself. The question isn't whether or not you are a good person, I'm sure you're an awesome person, but rather how a potential husband might perceive you from the outside. And please don't take this as me trying to tell you how to feel about yourself... I promise it's not like that at all. But I will keep it all the way real with you – the more you resist the truth behind the image in the mirror staring back at you, the harder it will be to find what you really want and be happy once you do.

Wife Material

I know there are some women who may view "kinkiness" in the bedroom as a contradiction to what a "good" woman stands for. And somehow believe that they will be viewed as less if they do certain things to please their man. Well, I'm here to tell you that this could not be further from the truth – at least in the eyes of men. And to answer the question that I'm sure is floating around in some of your heads – NO, love is not just about sex, however, sex is a big part of being in a relationship. It doesn't matter what you believe or how you feel about sex, the fact is that it brings some much needed balance to a love attachment in many ways. And for you "reserved" women out there, I have a solution for you. We all have heard of the "superhero" concept, stepping out of the norm and performing in a way that meets the needs of a particular situation. And although for the most part superhero's are not real, when it comes to you and your special someone, you can be anything you want to be. And NO, ladies… (for those of you making faces and funny "women" noises as you read along). I am not saying that you have to pull all types of crazy stunts to keep a smile on your man's face, because at the end of the day you want to do what works best for your relationship. And quite frankly… that ain't nunna mah bizness! But whatever it is that you *do* decide to do, remember to do it well enough to please him. And if you don't think *you* can, then that's where the "superhero" comes into play. And men, you have a part to play as well, and it's called patience. Not all women are the same, so if there is something you want then put it out there and give her time to come around. I'm sure even "Wonder Woman" had a hard time putting on her outfit the first time around. Look, I think I can speak for every man with confidence when I say that there is no feeling like coming home to a "superhero wonder woman" typa chick, who can save the day in so many ways (Help Me......Please...). When a man knows that the best part of his day is waiting at home he can't wait to get there. It gives a great sense of appreciation to know that he is special enough to have you come to his rescue, and not just anyone... but his one, his *superwoman*. And what happens at home is just that, what happens at home. No respect is lost when it comes to saving the day in your "City of Lovetroplis". I know I'm kind of geeking out with these super hero puns... but please just stay with me tho...

The Booth:

Just as much as you women want to feel sexy, we men want you to feel that way too, in fact, we want you to look sexy as well. Most men, whether they'll admit it to you or not, love it when his woman steps out looking like a million bucks with a killer pair of heels and a nice curve hugging dress – or even just some tight jeans and a tank top... *but with the heels too*. Don't be afraid to step out of the booth (so to speak) with the intentions of damn near breaking necks. Now let me be clear, although we men do appreciate a show of sex appeal in both public and private, we don't all get a kick out of an overly flirtatious groupie acting chick who jumps at every smile thrown her way... and no, please no, we don't want a "bitch" either. No one has time for a chick that's just too good for the world and not much sense to go with it. You cannot respect or appreciate anyone if you hold yourself in such high regard that no matter what a person does it'll never be good enough. And unless you change your evil ways, that's a recipe for a long and lonely life homegirl – so please... WAKE UP! Instead... we would rather have a "lady" with standards who knows what respect means for herself and her relationship. Just remember who you are, you are a super woman, and fellas, if your woman doesn't realize that she's your superwoman, wonder woman, or whatever superhero she needs to be, then you need to let her know. Women... you have the power to keep his jaw dropping every time he sees you, really... I don't care if you've been together for ten months or ten years. Find your booth and jump in! You need to know that a man not only wants but needs a superhero behind closed doors. Don't let anyone tell you different, not even him. He might be stuck in a shell himself and just needs for you to break him out. Once you guys have established something serious and he knows and respects who you are, I highly recommend that you let him meet his superhero. If there's one thing a man wants when considering a woman for the long term, it's the long term benefits. I don't mean to be crass but what good would my advice be if I were to dumb it down... I'm just saying...

Money Matters:

Love and money in the same sentence usually means "problem"... like divorce. And every day the world sees more and more of the two used together, and what it implies. As a very big and important part of building a successful relationship it would be foolish for anyone, man or woman, not to consider the importance of this topic. When it comes to a man considering a woman as a wife, a woman's head in the right place can really pay off... literally. And ladies, let's not twist any words here – you don't have to be a financial expert, that would just be overkill – but when money seems to flow in and out of your pockets like water you might want to step back and do a little self evaluating. Although this is not something that we men usually put at the forefront of conversations, however, the way a woman handles money is very important to us. Even men who make plenty money can appreciate a woman who is creative with her #bankflow. Either way you look at it, poor money management is not appealing in the least bit... man or woman. So the question now becomes; what exactly is considered positive behavior when it comes to women and money? A good balance is a very attractive trait when it comes to managing the finances. You ladies who can't seem to draw the line when it comes to shopping are considered "high-risk" (FYI) to most men. Maybe if a man finds you extremely attractive he might bend to win you over, but the problem is that he has to maintain the overtop spending that won you in the first place. Then the question for him becomes; why is she really with me? And although your purpose for being with him may not necessarily be the money, but by putting spending on such a high pedestal – you inevitably raise the question. No man sees a spendthrift woman as good wife material unless he is looking for someone to spoil... like a trophy wife, which I'm not saying is wrong at all. But I mean come on, we get what we pay for right, and if you have to pay for something it inevitably comes with conditions. So ladies, you want to be sure not to give off the impression that your love can be bought. Of course stability in the long run is important, but I don't think that can be determined by whether or not he can buy you those $1000 shoes.

The Attitude:

Your attitude is everything. It precedes you and has the power to draw in or scare off just about anyone. Just think of it as your advertisement – how do you want your commercial to look? Think about all the commercials you've seen on television that made you ask your friends if they'd seen it. How you present yourself displays to everyone what's inside, and just like the commercials, people are going to talk about it. So ladies... if you act crazy... how many men in their right mind do you think will see you as wife material? And for you women who believe that a nasty attitude earns you respect, I've got news for you... That type of attitude only creates eggshells and a reason for a man to either avoid or abandon a relationship with you... acting like you ain't got no damn sense. Furthermore, being nice does not mean letting someone run over you. If you find a man who's not about anything then it won't matter whether you are sweet as pie or sour as a lemon, he's not going to change – at least not until he's ready. In fact, acting like you have no sense will only create bigger problems for you in the long run. This is because if he's trying to get something out of you, his game will go into overdrive to avoid detection by the "angry girl". I doubt anyone reading this right now wants to be with an angry person, right? If I'm wrong send me an email and I'll see what I can do to get you on a reality t.v. show… sike, I'm just playin'… But seriously, you should always be the type of person you expect from others. How can you expect or see it as okay to want a well rounded lover when you are only half-rounded? Please understand and know that I'm not passing any judgment here… I'm not perfect, not in the least, nor is anyone reading this book. However, that doesn't mean because you've got flaws that you should just write it off as…_just the way it is_. If you know that your attitude needs adjusting then you need to do something about it. Go talk to someone, read a book, find a counselor, a preacher, a friend, or whoever – do whatever it takes, just don't do _nothing_.

Before anyone can be real with you and take you seriously, you need to do the same with yourself – keep it real and make your personal growth a priority. One of the best ways of identifying your areas of opportunity when it comes to the opposite sex is asking the opposite sex. Of course you want to use your own common sense and experiences as well, but you can't count out the other side. This will also give you a chance to better connect with that special someone. So don't be afraid to communicate, even at the expense of your own ego. The right attitude will not only make way for the right person in your life, but also a lot of other things as well.

Handling Hers

-Get It Right

A woman about hers understands the difference between *getting* a man and *keeping* one. Any woman can get a man, that's not really a hard thing to do. Keeping a man is something altogether different. When I talk about "hers" I don't mean a woman with a nasty attitude or a chip on her shoulder. For whatever reason, women, and even men in some instances, think in order for a woman to be independent she has to always push back against being open, or nice, or anything else pleasant when it comes to men. A woman about hers isn't invincible to pain, however, she does not allow the struggles of life to hold her down. She handles her problems with grace and courage and doesn't let them take her over. To be about yours first begins with you... having respect for yourself and not allowing the world to dictate how you see yourself, whether beautiful or not. But you won't know this until you try it. Look in the mirror without all that stuff you've added to yourself... make-up, hair, clothes... and keep looking until you learn to love what you see. You can get all the education in the world, the best job, the best house, best car, but you can never buy love for yourself. You can only allow it to be.

Musiq

-Keep Calm

If a man feels all roughed up after an encounter with you as though he's dealing with a drill sergeant, then that's not a good sign. Although he may not tell you that you make him feel that way, trust me he does. When you come across all extra angry there's only one reaction a person can have to that – unless they're crazy. And ladies, a good way to tell if you have this impact on him is to pay attention to his actions. If you notice while talking to him that he avoids a certain topic that caused you to go off before, that's a sure sign that he's trying to avoid the fire. There are a lot of ways a man might respond to drill sergeant like behavior, just look for any discomfort in his body language. Ask any man what he thinks about a polite woman who knows how to treat people and has the ability to manage her emotions, love herself, and go for what she wants. What man wouldn't want her by his side?

-Her Man

At the end of the day we all need love... man or woman, there are no exceptions. In all honestly you ladies have the power to make men feel like "Superman" before we ever graduate superhero school... and trust me, we know from the jump what qualities you are bringing to the table. Unfortunately, just like you, men sometimes settle too – whether for convenience, looks, or any number of reasons that might cause him to choose poorly. Being aware of your part when it comes to making your man happy and what that means will make a huge difference in your relationship – trust me. As a man, by nature I'm pretty simple when it comes to being pleased. And to make sure I hold it down for all men and keep things simple I came up with four words that I like to call the *"simple four"*. The purpose behind these words is to help both sides win and not just the men. And by win I'm talking about your love life. But don't expect every man to appreciate what I'm about to share with you – because no matter what you do, if he's on some other stuff, there's not much that can be done to change his mind. And while I'm on changing minds let me say this; PLEASE STOP TRYING TO CHANGE GROWN PEOPLE'S MINDS. It's a waste of time and will only put off and or prolong your suffering. The simple four:

- Support
- Sex
- Space
- Spontaneity

When it all adds up the simple four is everything we've talked about so far. Of course it was tailored for the men so ladies you might want to get out your pen and paper and take some notes. Just remember to stick to the script and keep it simple!

Support
From the mouth of a man I will tell you that a woman worth taking serious is one who doesn't mind showing her support. And I don't mean just compliments,

Musiq

I'm also talking about being down for him through whatever challenges come up. Support in any case is good, but there's nothing like showing love when love is all there is to give. If what you have is worth it, or when you find yourself in a situation that's worth it, give all of your support and watch the good it does for your relationship.

Sex

Taking care of home is more than just cleaning up and cooking a good meal here and there. Maintaining an intimate connection with that special someone has all kinds of benefits... we've talked about it some already so I won't take up too much time on the subject. But I don't think it's possible to stress it enough – a happy home will always include good "love making". And anyone out there who might see this as a bad thing, I have to wonder if the sex is any good in your relationship. All I'm saying is take care of home and home will take care of you.

Space

It's not that we don't love you or don't want to spend time with you, but most men without a doubt need their space. And I know this is not just a guy thing, because we all need space to avoid feeling smothered. Too much of being in one another's face 25/8 has a way of turning sour. Don't take away from him the things that existed before you came along. Whether he's into sports, video games, or whatever, don't kill his flame. You shouldn't take his need for space personally, but rather as a contribution to the longevity of your love.

Spontaneity

Being spontaneous is something people always talk about but can't seem to do or keep up. Needless to say, life can get a little crazy and finding time to always do something new can be hard. To be honest, most people make the whole act of being spontaneous into more than what it really is. Ladies, as you know us men are pretty simple, so it doesn't take much to light us up. That's not to down men in any way... just keeping it real. And when I say simple, I mean simple. Let's say you cook his favorite meal – throw in something extra like maybe his favorite drink, or anything else he might appreciate along with it. You don't have to do much, just do something a little different when you can. And it never hurts to personalize whatever it is you come up with. Think about his favorite color, or sports team, or car, or hobby... etc... not that you'll be able to customize what you do every time, just keep it in mind for when you can.

The point is, every relationship is different and your job is to pay attention to the needs of your situation. The start of a good relationship begins with each person. If you can't get yourself right then not much else is going to work out for you. So ladies, standout and separate yourself from the nonsense so that the right man can notice you, and from there you will just have to see...

CHAPTER

THE TYPE pt.2

Buddy Status & A Problem

Buddy Status

A buddy is a friend with benefits.... and before I continue let me explain what I mean by "benefits". The "benefits" of your friendship or "Buddy Status" can be whatever you and the other person decides. However the two of you come to whatever understanding of this is completely up to you. Every situation will require a different definition depending on the relationship. If being a buddy makes you happy then go for it, I am neither condemning nor condoning. If it means just hanging out, talking about life stuff, and exchanging emotional experiences, cool. If it means all of the above with a little sex every now and again, fine. Even if it means sex with some other stuff thrown in here and there 'cause y'all cool, whatever, as long as you *both* agree to those terms. Not sayin' you gotta have a city hall meeting about it, just let it be known what you want, and be very clear about it. The other person deserves an opportunity to say yay or nay! I mean look... It's your life and you should be able to live it however you choose, just be sure not to confuse that role with anything else and then get mad when it doesn't work out. Make sure that the other person involved is aware of their "Buddy Status", and yes, there are plenty of women who never received the buddy-memo when it was passed out. If you do find yourself as someone's buddy, just remember that it takes two and that's what I want to talk about.

-What's Really Good

Although I don't want to come across as though I am making excuses for any man who tags his female friend as a buddy – I *do* want to call both sides out and stress the importance to the ladies on how not to end up on the buddy list. Sometimes men go actively looking for a certain type of woman, while other times... *most* times, a woman just may show up in a man's life. For a woman, giving off the right signals is important because you never know who you're meeting and what they're about. How you carry yourself tells a man whether or not your standards are set and locked in, or if your just another pretty face with a nice body. And this doesn't stop after you first meet. You don't want to come across as bitchy... no... however, you *definitely* don't want to come across as a woman who doesn't really respect herself or knows her true worth. No matter how sweet you are as a person, when you don't set the proper tone you might find yourself with more of the wrong men chasing you or cause them to not take you serious. You should note that you will only be taken as seriously as you take yourself.

-Auto Profiling

Anytime someone crosses our path we can give at least a general rundown of what they are about. You can call it stereotyping if you want, but the truth of the matter is... we all do it! This doesn't mean you shouldn't give someone a chance based on how they may look when you meet them. What if they just got off work or some crazy situation like my man Will Smith in "The Pursuit of Happiness" before the interview? They could have easily dismissed him but didn't and because of that made big money together. But not everyone is willing to take that risk, especially when it comes to hooking up with the opposite sex. As for men, most of us struggle with society and how a "good girl" should look and act. So between whether or not he feels comfortable taking you home to mom, or being clowned by his boys for "wifing a hoochie", choosing a potential wife is sometimes a bigger decision than just his.

-First Intentions

Another issue is when he wants to have his cake and eat it too. No matter what the outside pressures are, if he thinks you're sexy then he's going to want to have sex with you. Now you have a situation where he talks a good game just to get in, and after he's *in* his intention doesn't go past sex. At this point you are officially his buddy. And as if this wasn't bad enough, women often stick around and remain the buddy even when they know good and well they should move on. And if it helps at all, it's no coincidence when a man doesn't want to marry you because "he's not ready" – then right after you break up he pulls a complete three-sixty and marries the next woman he gets with. More times than not the next woman either looks a certain way or carries certain qualities that you don't. In situations like this he was more than likely just killing time until he found what he wanted. Either way he doesn't deserve you crying over him.

-How Did We Get Here

Now, ladies, you can't fix the world or the confused men you might come across, but what you *can* do is not put yourself in harm's way – and either avoid or keep the wrong men away. When it comes to the whole buddy thing, there are two categories that men fall into. First is the guy with the right intentions but for whatever reason acts against his better judgment and interests. Second is the one who considers himself a player, aka "Big Pimpin", and only really wanted one thing from the jump. You should already know how to handle no.2... But the first one might end up deciding against a long-term relationship, but would still struggle to pull away because of the sex or something else he doesn't want to let go of. Regardless of how you end up as someone's buddy, the only way it can continue is if you allow it to. Any man, no matter his intentions, knows when a woman will go for being a buddy. Maybe at first she will talk a good game and swear up and down that she could never become some man's side toy – and then later find herself lost in her emotions and unable to break free. My point is not just about showing you what not to do in order to avoid the buddy situation, but also how to deal with the situation if you ever find yourself there. When a man with the wrong intentions sees a woman he likes, he's going to look for any signs that he can try her. If you come across as easy, transparent, lacking opinion, acting like a groupie or money hungry – it's obvious that your standards may not be the highest and with a little game, money, or both he can slide right in. On the other hand, let's say he thought he wanted something with you and for whatever reason changes his mind... however, he doesn't want to walk away just yet because maybe he doesn't want to see you with someone else before he moves on, or some other reason that might make him not want to leave. If you find yourself with a guy who wants to have his cake and eat it too, there will be all types of red flags to tell you that he's dragging you along. A red flag for instance might be other women, and even if he's not doing it intentionally, he just might be on auto-pilot and waiting on someone else to come along – who'll inevitably replace you.

-My Buddy

If you think I'm saying that the "Buddy Status" makes a woman out to be some kind of messed up in the head chick... then I apologize 'cause you'd be very, very wrong. Like I said before, just because a woman finds herself as a man's "buddy" doesn't mean that she's a bad person. She may be a little misguided or something of that nature but she's not the devil. But when a woman keeps ending up on the buddy train without necessarily wanting to be there, then it's more than likely *her* just as much as the men she's dealing with. If this is you, a little self reflection may be needed to find out what's going on inside emotionally. The quality of your love life when it's all said and done is up to you, don't forget that.

A Problem

For the women who believe that an over the top attitude is the answer... I wrote this for you and all the ladies on the verge of becoming "A Problem"... I want to do whatever I can to help. Not only does it make you look crazy, it can also become extremely unhealthy for both yourself and whatever man you bring into your life. Not to mention it blocks true happiness and anything else good that could possibly come out of a relationship. Trying to stay ahead of the curve by acting crazy and stressing a man out won't get you anywhere good... AT ALL! You might get what you want for a little while or maybe even longer, but in the end no one will be happy. You cannot pressure a man into becoming something that he's not. If you can't accept him for who he is then you don't need to be with him. A woman who's "A Problem" is good for blaming others for *her* problems when truthfully the PROBLEM *is* her. If something is off or missing on the inside, the outside will always suffer. When it comes to relationships any man in your life will become, if not already, the target of unrealistic expectations, ridicule, insults, judgment, and a whole list of other things. If this is you... then I highly recommend that after you finish reading this book to revisit Act I and focus on getting yourself ready for love. And since we're on the topic, I want to go a little deeper from a man's point of view in support of both sexes, so we can get this right.

Ladies, for those of you who fall into this category the worst thing you can do is deny it. I mean let's face it, probably by now you've been running from something your whole life, in one way or another, so why keep running. If you want to correct whatever it is that makes you act out toward men in the way that you do, then you have to stand up and put some real effort into fighting against it. I came up with a list of what I call "Problematic Tendencies" to be more specific. This pertains to women who are usually or at least more often than not:

- Judgmental
- Self righteous
- Extremely Moody
- Feisty
- Unrealistic with her expectations
- Unforgiving
- All about the perfect man when she's not perfect herself
- All about being "wifed-up" but can't seem to act like one

Just like the "Buddy" type, "A Problem" is more than likely good people with good intentions, however, somewhere along the way things kind of went wrong. Generally, what went wrong happened so long ago, maybe even as far back as childhood. And I know that so many of you women have found yourself on the receiving end of something that may have negatively impacted you at some point in your life. And I am not looking to make excuses for you, but there is a root cause somewhere, and it's in your best interest to find it if you ever you want to find your way out of the pain. And I call it pain because that's exactly what it is. I know that no woman likes the way acting crazy makes her feel. When you know your attitude is messed up and you see the pain caused after the fact, then you need to do something about it. Although I'm not a woman I can totally empathize with this because as men we struggle with our own things. If you want to know the truth about how your actions impact the man in your life, just ask him. The goal here is not about calling anyone out or making them feel guilty, I don't want ANYONE to feel guilty. I just want you to take what I'm saying and if you KNOW that you need to work on yourself then please, just be honest about it and get to work. No need to sit around and hope that the right man will come along who can put up with you and your shit... I mean, you might be able to find someone to put up with you for a minute, but it's going to cost, not just the person you're with, but you, your family and friends, too. Ask yourself how happy do you think you or anyone can be when so much pain stands in the way of your heart? The phrase "soul searching" comes to mind... so get searching.

EXAMPLE: PART 10 (STATUS UPGRADE)

After taking another sip of her coffee Stacey asks Monica what she would like a man to think when he sees her on the street, at work, or wherever. Monica states that she wants a man to see her and think of her as "wife material". Stacey responds back and asks her how men generally react to her when they meet. After pondering the question for several seconds, Monica shrugs her shoulders and says that she isn't completely sure. She admits to getting many different responses from men but always end up walking away empty handed. Stacey pushes the cup forward and leans back in her chair.

"Monica... before I respond, let me just say that no matter the situation I will always relate the solution to *any* issues that you may have – and how they impact the way you go about looking for love. Now, when it comes to men they are going to try you, this is a fact. And if you don't believe me take a trip to any bar or gym..."

Monica nods her head in agreement. Stacey continues.

"There are three main categories I have for women when it comes to dating and they are; Wife Material, Buddy Status, and A Problem. For starters, a woman who's Wife Material would NEVER settle for or even let herself become some man's plaything, because her standards and commitment to those standards will not allow it to happen – or if she finds herself in a "Buddy" situation she will quickly exit. *Unlike* many women who end up as a buddy for years and years, the "wife type" understands that you cannot force a man to want you. Worst case scenario – if she learns that a man who she thought was about something is actually not, she will simply cut her losses and leave, and a man who is just after the "benefits" will less likely put up a big enough fight and go the distance with her. I mean, regardless of the game he puts out there, either you're going to accept playing the role of dummy or you're not, it's just that simple." Her response brings a smile to Michael's face as he waits to hear more.

"The last one to mention is the "Problem" type. This woman reeks of self-righteousness and thinks that an angry and crazy attitude is the solution to whatever issues she has with men. Of course we all know such women get nowhere and end up right back where they started. And another thing you should consider is that once you *do* have the right man, be sure to take care of him, and what I mean by that is accepting him for **who he is**... don't try changing him. If you feel that he needs to be changed then you probably don't need to be with him. And I'm not talking about small changes like the way he dresses... although that too can sometimes become an issue."

CHAPTER

GOOD MAN

Finding Him, Loving Him, and Him Being Good to You

Musiq

When it comes to finding love you have to also consider maintaining that love – and this goes for both sides. If you're looking for something that you don't plan on giving in return then you are a hypocrite, and really don't deserve anything more. There are too many people complaining about what they don't get out of relationships instead of looking at what they can put into one. On your journey to finding someone to call yours, be prepared to love and set your standards high and demand love in return. And I know that demand is a strong word – but shouldn't you expect to be loved and appreciated in a relationship? If you could... not saying that you should... but if you *could* put a dollar amount on your worth, wouldn't you want to get every penny? Don't sell yourself short here. No matter which side we're talking about, man or woman, both sides must throw in their lot. Men tend to live by sexist double standards, and please understand that I don't mean *every* man. But for those who fall into this category, how're you going to have all these demands when it comes to wanting 'Wife Material" yet you're the complete opposite of what *you* want in a woman? Come on man... I need for those of you living and thinking this way to get it right. It's not right to expect the perfect woman when you aren't perfect yourself. There are always two sides to a situation, and that means men holding themselves to higher standards as well. Coming together as one means working together, building together, and healing together. Don't expect anything to be together until you understand what it takes to make "together" happen.

Fellas, I'm going to take a moment and speak to the ladies but I need for you to stay put and read along. I think that everything, when it comes to love, is the business of both men and women. The purpose of this chapter is about finding, loving, and being a good man. First, I'm going to talk about finding a good man – which basically covers how you ladies can go about finding the kind of guy that works and will do right by you. Second, is loving that man – which talks about the things that come after you find him. And third, for the men – how to be a good man. Not that I'm saying you don't know how, but I think it's important to talk about it because in doing so you might learn a thing or two that might reveal some flaws in your own mode of operation. I also want to give the ladies a man's point of view on what I feel you all deserve from men.

–Finding Her

Okay, here we have a two way street that requires the active participation of both sexes. Being found is all about being available and while you're at it, why not make sure that you look the part as well. I mean, I don't want to tell anyone how to dress or act, just don't get mad when you get passed up for giving off the wrong impression. This is not about changing who you are, but rather preparing yourself to find and get the woman you want. There's somebody for everyone, don't forget that, so don't be afraid to be who you are. And one more thing before I speak to the ladies – if a woman is not into your style or what have you, don't take it personal. Some men can be super selective and then get mad when they themselves aren't selected.

—Finding Him

Now ladies, as far as finding a man goes, you have to be mindful of how you go about doing this. This includes the where, the how, the this, the that, and so on. If you keep experiencing the same kind of dudes, then you must be doing something to attract them. Ask yourself what type of signals am I sending out there to attract a particular type of man. Or maybe it's the places you hang out *or* the most common which is, when the type of man you claim to want presents himself and you shoot him down. Maybe you think that something "new" might not keep you satisfied, but just keep in mind that you could be wrong. Being afraid to broaden your perspective and adopting a new list of options when it comes to men is a perfect recipe for "Oh I just can't find the right man for me!". And *this is true*, but what you *should* do if this is you is remove everything else but the "I" and there you will find your answer. As far as what you ladies should be looking for, I can only go so far with that one because in the end it's up to you. If there's a ditch ten feet ahead and I say "there's a ditch up ahead, watch your step" it's on you what you do with the information.

Let's assume that your decision making when it comes to the opposite sex is a little biased. Breaking these types of patterns can be hard because a brain hardwired to like a certain thing is not easy to undo. So I put together a list to hopefully help those of you in need. This list is designed to help you focus on the most important things –

the type of things that don't have you asking yourself; "what the hell was I thinking" after six months of suffering. So ladies, when you are looking for a man, look for "A MAN", not a title – for example... you shouldn't just go looking for a doctor, or a lawyer, or ball player. I know a stable companion is never a bad thing, but stability can't buy love. So if you want love, then act like it, anything else is just an excuse to keep making bad decisions. When choosing someone to be with think about what your priorities are. And you might have a good reason for having those priorities – but ask yourself are they realistic and aligned with your long-term goal for happiness. I am not knocking anyone for wanting to have a stable situation – I mean, you have to think about the future, you guys might want to start living together or have children some day, or maybe you already do. There's a lot to consider when making a big decision like being with someone – this could be your life partner. My point is that when making your decision don't base it on the wrong things like titles and other nonsense. You will never find true happiness that way, so maybe if you consider the following you just might...

Quality

So let's say a young lady (who we'll call Tina) meets a guy (who we'll call Will) who looks the part. He's not dressed all crazy or acting like he's still in High School. His behavior says that he's mature and has a stable head on his shoulders. Will asks for her number and she thinks; "why not, I'm single and I think this dude is alright". Tina gives him the number and he calls later to set up a date. A week later they meet for dinner and have a great time. And although she usually goes for the more "rugged" type, she doesn't allow that to stand in the way. Tina is pleased with the quality of what she's found, and now puts her mind to his stability and potential.

Stability/Potential

As far as an occupation, Will is building a new business from the ground up. He is about a year and a half in and using his savings from a previous job to pay the bills. He has secured some promising deals, although financially he is not in the clear just yet. He's not able to splurge and do much of what Tina is used to from dating other men, but he *can* do the basics and has transportation to get back and forth. Tina is impressed by his drive and decides against her unnecessarily expensive habits, and instead asks what she can do to contribute. Being that she does not have a lot of money herself, she offers to make calls on behalf of the business and help out with paperwork. Will is glad because he needs the help but cannot afford to pay anyone at the moment.

Vanity

From the very start Tina was attracted to Will, although she did not particularly care for his less than flashy style. He didn't wear designer jeans or shoes – although he rocked a killer suit when handling business. In time she grew to appreciate his style and even gave him some advice to help out with his dress habits. She could've easily allowed his image to be a deal breaker but didn't. The fact that the exterior sometimes reflects what's on the inside is a legit reason to consider a person's appearance. But she wasn't looking to change him at all, instead simply suggested a few things, giving a little advice every now and then which ultimately helped to enhance his overall swag – and he was grateful for the upgrade. Now she can't take her eyes off of him no matter what he wears.

In the end Will's company went on to generate millions over the coming years and he finally asked for her to marry him, and she said yes. Although they were an unlikely couple at first, her open mindedness allowed her the chance to get to know him and learn to appreciate who he was. When it came to certain extravagances that she was used to, she put them down just a little lower on her list of priorities, because she knew by putting quality first that she would find a meaningful relationship. She learned from previous situations that by putting the wrong things first, like money and material things, that she would never find lasting happiness. Tina allowed herself to "find him" by moving out of her own way. Had she decided against Will because he didn't fit her "typical" profile, then she would have missed out on something great. So the point is this, ladies, when looking for that special man don't just look – first find YOU, and for your own good get out of your own way and see where it takes you.

–Loving Him

After you've found him, now what? Just like you guys want us to keep it up, we men want the same. And if your man is not "keeping it up"… take that however you want… then you need to handle that. We're going to talk more about what "he" should be doing next. I don't want to come across as if having a man is a job, because it's not and no woman is any man's slave, but it *is* sort of like that. Look at it like this – when you go apply for a job and tell the interviewer all this great stuff about you – do you just quit working once they hire you? No… or at least I hope not. Although some people do and those people get fired. A good start is only as good as your intentions to follow through. If you recall a couple chapters back we talked about the whole "superhero" act – well, let's just say this is "cat woman's" queue to leap into action. Just so long as he's acting right you should always treat the situation like you're working for a promotion. And that means always be on time, adhere to the company's code of conduct, and meet your stats. All else is "fire me" behavior.

–Being Him

Now fellas… not that I want to give you all a hard time, I mean, why would I do that – I'm a man. So everything I say comes right back on me *too*. But I do want to bring some balance to the discussion because a lot of us don't seem to get the "balance" part. You have to stay up on your *"A-Game"* at ALL times gentlemen! And I don't mean just in the bedroom. Sex with your lady is a happy time, true, but should not be treated like happy hour or a fix–it–all. And that goes double for you ladies, y'all know exactly what I'm talking about. And please don't play dumb because I know better – *and I love you all but you ain't slick… and I'll leave it at that*…. But getting back to the men – YOU can't just wait until the end of the week to be excited and show some appreciation for your woman. Don't forget about Monday through Thursday. When you sign up to love you need to show up, it's just that simple. If you're intentions are to play games then let that be known because believe it or not, as crazy as it may sound, there are many women out there who are up for that, too. "Being Him" or a being good man, however you want to phrase it, means living up to what you claim to represent. You don't have to be perfect or have a lot of money, but you *do* need to stand by your word. In defense of men in general I feel that society places a lot of pressure to perform when it comes to money and other things that should never be put first when building a relationship. And as a result, women find themselves following the same trend. So now you have two people with crooked priorities trying to form a straight line and build something real... I'm sorry y'all but it's just never going to work. And just like it's up to women to break away from the nonsense society feeds them, we men must do the same. And the best way to start is by first keeping it real with yourself. Don't go out trying to be what you think women want. The most attractive thing anybody can be is themselves. I have three points that I want to make when it comes to "Being Him":

Know Who You Are

First things first, you have to know who you are. If you don't know who you are then you will find yourself trying to be any and everything but YOU. You will waste time trying to impress women with material stuff alone and still come up empty handed because the appreciation was never for you but instead what you have. This is how guys get into trouble by trying to keep up with the next man when it comes to cars and all that other irrelevant stuff. Who you are has nothing to do with material things, so why balance your confidence and self respect on something that you could lose any day?

Appreciate Who You Are

The next and very important thing is to appreciate who you are. We all know that no matter how many sneakers we buy, cars we drive, houses we own, or whatever, that it will not bring lasting happiness. When you appreciate who you are, nothing on the outside can add or take away from your happiness. Yeah, of course it's cool to do a little shopping and have nice things, make constant contributions to your "baller" status in the name of being "fresh"... but when you do those things to feel good then you're really *not* good... not on the inside at least.

Be Who You Are

When you know and appreciate who you are, only then can you truly *be* who you are. This part is so important when it comes to relationships. If you haven't figured out who you are yet, which can be said for a lot of men... trust me I know... then how in the world do you expect to be who "she" needs you to be in a relationship? God forbid she's all mixed up in the head herself. That's when we get two people who shouldn't have kids together or anything else for that matter!

Remember, to get love you have to give it, and to give it you have to know how. It's never good to just go through the motions in a relationship. You end up wasting your time, the other person's, and if kids are involved you end up setting a bad example for them. I can't tell anyone how to go about love because it's your own thing. But I do know that when it comes to those key pieces like communication and so on, that by not acting in the best interest of your relationship that it will soon dry up and fade away. Don't let this be the pattern for your life. Find you, find love, and I wish you and your heart the very best...

Musiq

EXAMPLE: PART 11 (WHAT KIND OF MAN WILL YOU BE)

Turning her attention to Michael, Stacey asks him what he thinks it means to be a good man. Glancing down, Michael takes a moment to process the question before he responds.

"Well, my mother always told me to respect women and love my family. I think if you know how to do those things then everything else will kind of fall into place."

Stacey nods and crosses her legs. Exhaling she locks her fingers and wraps them around her upraised knee.

"Well Michael, I do agree with the first part of what you said, but to think that everything will just *'fall in place'* because you show respect is a recipe for disaster. When it comes to men and their 'role' in society, you should remember three things: 1...Know who you are, 2...Appreciate who you are, and 3...Be who you are. The knowing means that you don't measure your worth based on monetary value. When men do this it usually leads to putting up a show and losing all sense of who they are. Women don't like this and can see right through it. Even worse, there are many women who will play up to a man who thinks that way and take advantage of him. When you cannot be real with yourself you will never get real results when it comes to love or even life in general. And knowing who you are means very little if you do not appreciate it. Without the appreciation the knowing part is covered up with all the material crap that I mentioned before. Men who are afraid to approach a woman they like unless they have a nice car – or disguise themselves with diamonds and all that stuff in order to catch a woman's attention is basically asking to be taken advantage of. And please understand that there are some *very* clever and crafty chicks out here, and will NOT hesitate to take you for everything you're worth. I find that the underlining truth behind these types of men is that the real person, in their mind, is not good enough and therefore requires a little extra. And when a man doesn't feel good enough he can't *be* good enough, at least not without his money, cars, or jewelry. This is why when any of those things are lost such men panic and sometimes fall into a depression because they've now become vulnerable and exposed, in their minds. Lastly, when you know who you are and appreciate who you are, you can be who you are. Ask any woman and they will tell you that there is nothing more attractive than a man who knows who he is. But you will never know until you expose and accept yourself and all that comes with it."

Monica looks down at her watch. "Oh my god I can't believe what time it is! I have to run and pick up my daughter." Stacey hurries to her feet to let Monica out of the building. Michael grabs his jacket and follows. As Monica makes her way out the door to her car Michael exits with her. He waves his cousin goodbye as he sees Monica to her car. Going into his pocket he pulls out his business card and thanks her for allowing him to join the discussion. She smiles as she lowers herself into the car. The car cranks and Michael steps back. Still holding the card in his hand he hesitates and then steps forward and taps on her window. Stacey watches through the glass of her office door. Monica rolls down her window and regards Michael's extended hand with a smile. Surprised, she slowly reaches out and grabs the card. Unsure of what to make of it, she searches his face for signs of mischief as she neatly places the card into her purse. Shifting the gear in reverse she backs out and waves bye. Through the window she gestures with her hand that she will call as she drives off. A more than excited Michael smiles and waves her goodbye.

BONUS CHAPTER

LOVE LESSONS

Musiq

As an added bonus I wanted to take some time to go over some simple yet BIG ways to keep the flame burning bright in your relationship. As cliché as it sounds, people always take for granted the small stuff. It's like one of those things that's so easy and low maintenance, yet seems to be such a challenge for people to keep up. For those of you who don't know, you'd be surprised by how far a small gesture can go. Birthdays, holidays, and other special days are fun, no doubt – but when you think of someone as your lover, I think it's fair to say that they deserve to be acknowledged on more than just special occasions. And I'm not saying that you have to constantly spend money as if it were a special occasion, because you don't. Sometimes the simplest things have the greatest impact. So I came up with a list of what I think are easy and effective ways to bring a smile to a lover's face without going broke or taking up an entire day:

–Smile

What better way to begin the day than with a smile? It grabs a person's attention and brightens up their day even before the sun rises. Many of you probably met after an exchange of smiles. We've been doing it since we were babies because it's natural. Even before we knew what it was we knew that it felt good. So why would we not use it as much as possible when we can? If there's anything we should smile about... shouldn't it be love...?

STOP!

Excuse me... I hate to interrupt the flow of your reading, but right now I need for you to put down the book, get up and go tell someone you love them! Don't worry, I can wait... And if you're wondering why... check the page number...

...aight... *continue...*

Musiq

−Kiss

If that special someone is into kissing, then do it! It doesn't cost you a penny... at any exchange rate... and you always get something out of it − almost like getting something for nothing. A kiss is simple yet powerful at the same time. It can mean *and* do a whole bunch of things... like wishing them a good day, telling them you're glad to see them, or just reminding them that someone in this world thinks that they're special. And you can do it at any time you feel the need. In the morning when you wake up, throughout the day when you guys are out and about, maybe at lunch or a movie, or just chillin at night before bed. But you don't have to stop there, the list goes on; it could be all in public, your mommas house... whenever, wherever, whatever... it's at your disposal so don't hesitate to put it to use...

−Touch

A simple touch can say a million things and like a kiss it costs you absolutely nothing. And furthermore, just like a kiss, it can be done just about anywhere. You can do it in the car, at the mall, the gym, at church... you get the idea. And for those of you with gutter brains I'm *not* talking about sex, or anything like that. When I say touch, I'm talking about something as simple as placing your hand on her shoulder, a light graze at the small of her back, or gentle squeeze on her thigh... not to mention holding hands or finding a reason to pick at her clothes for lint. Come on people, y'all know what I'm talkin' bout...

−Simple gift

A simple gift can be anything from a candy bar to a dandelion picked from the yard... I know the dandelion one is a little corny but so what. It ain't about the damn dandelion, it's about the meaning behind it. Just find out what your special someone likes and start creating. It's only corny if you don't know what they like. If you're with someone who loves rocks go find a couple of cool rocks and give it to them. If they're a collector then take it a step further and go by Wal-mart or somewhere like that and find a display case to put the rock in. Again, you practically end up paying just about nothing, but to the person on the receiving end it might as well be a brand new car. And yeah, yeah I know... a new car *would* be nice... but that's *sooo* not the point people...

−Reminders

Reminders can be anything from a text, to a poem, to actually telling someone that you love them. We all get busy in our daily lives but that's never an excuse to not take a couple minutes and do something, or say something... anything. Every moment is another chance to remind your man or woman that you love them. And of course you can't spend every minute reminding someone how you feel about them, because if you did they would probably leave in fear of you being clingy, emotionally unstable, or just crazy. The point I want to make is that no time is a bad time, so if you want to do something then do it. If you want to say something then say it, even if YOU don't really want to at

145

that point in time. If you KNOW it would make them feel good, or at least a little bit better about their day, then why not. You're not in the relationship with just yourself. You *do* realize that there's someone else in it with you... right?

–Special Time
      The last thing that I want to mention is time. You should always be willing to make time for that special someone. And I'm including myself in this as well;

IT DOES NOT MATTER WHAT IS GOING ON IN YOUR LIFE, YOU CAN ALWAYS FIND TIME TO SPEND WITH THE ONE YOU LOVE... IF YOU REALLY WANT TO!

I know firsthand how challenging it can be to find some time, so I promise you... I GET IT!!! However, there will always be what I like to call "pockets of time" throughout your day. Make it your business to schedule a moment or two to let that special someone know how important they are to you. Even if it's just a simple phone conversation, no text messages, no emails. Call them and give more than just a "what's up". Find out what's *really* up, how their day is going, you never know what a person may be dealing with. And of course when you can, try squeezing in a vacation here and there. You might not be able to go a month, but you can at least shoot for a couple days. Just remember, what may seem small to you in terms of time could mean the world to the other person. And lastly, special time does not include your family and friends... sorry!

FINAL EXAMPLE: AT LAST

(The Story of Michael and Monica)

They have a relationship that is thorough, based on the principles presented throughout this book.

TWO YEARS LATER...

Truly amazed and proud of herself, Monica reclines in the patio chair on the back deck of her and Michael's new home. Proudly wearing a three karat engagement ring, she reflects on life as it used to be compared to now. Never in a million years did she believe that such a wonderful man would want to marry her. Not only was he successful and handsome, but extremely loving and caring. Everything that she's ever wanted but never thought was possible was literally right under her nose the entire time. She even learned that some years back they had attended some of the same family functions at Stacey's home. Most importantly, she understood that none of this would be possible if she had not been able to accept herself. Despite the challenges she faced through her up-bringing she was able to overcome, but not before realizing that the real war was within.

Musiq

The backdoor opens as Michael makes his way out onto the patio. He kisses her on the forehead before taking the chair next to her. With a clear understanding of loving themselves and one another, the very things that were once considered to be problems became opportunities. Michael had fully accepted Monica's past and instead of criticizing her, he praised her for being so strong and coming through on top. Monica's habit of taking out past hurt on her current man had long died out as she focused on herself and what it meant to fully and truly love someone else.

A Note from Musiq

No matter who you are or what you've been through, true love is at your disposal. And although my experience with some situations may be limited, it's my understanding of love that I rely on. Being a good lover involves more than just the bedroom, but also how we interact and take care of one another every day. No matter your current situation or soon to be one, when you know love, you know yourself, and when you know yourself you can love someone else. Before then, no matter how many men or women you have married, dated, kissed, or whatever, you aren't feeding real love but instead what you THINK is love – and that can be mistaken for anything, and often is. This is why when things get a little crazy, financially or otherwise, very few people ever make it through. This is because it was never true and honest love. I wish you the very best in your love life and hope that my words have encouraged you to love more, love harder, AND love smarter. Many thanks, blessings and much love... *143*

-Musiq Soulchild

THE CONVERSATION: LOVE TALK

What's up everyone! The conversation, aka Love Talk, is a platform for lovers, friends, and whoever else wants to talk about LOVE... Whoever you decide to invite along, be sure to have a mixture of both sexes in order to get the most out of it. No real progress can be made with a group of just men or just women beating up on the opposite sex. This section is made up of each chapter with questions about what was discussed. Now it's your turn to write, express, and talk about how you feel about love and relationships. Let's go!

CHAPTER 1: LOVE

🎵 *Is it possible for an emotionally damaged person to succeed in love?* 🎵

_____

_____

_____

_____

_____

_____

_____

_____

_____

Musiq

🎵 *When it comes to relationships what things do you believe stand in the way of happiness?* 🎵

_____

_____

_____

_____

_____

_____

_____

_____

_____

_____

_____

🎵 *Do you believe that unconditional love in today's world is possible?* 🎵

_____

_____

_____

_____

_____

_____

_____

_____

_____

_____

_____

_____

Musiq

CHAPTER 2: COMMUNICATION

🎵 *On a scale from 1 to 10, with 10 being the highest, how would you rate your communication?* 🎵

_____

_____

_____

_____

_____

_____

_____

_____

_____

_____

_____

🎵*On the same scale as the previous question, how does your man or woman rate your communication?* 🎵

_____

_____

_____

_____

_____

_____

_____

_____

_____

_____

_____

Musiq

🎵*How do you feel about their response and if necessary what are you going to do about it?*🎵

_____

_____

_____

_____

_____

_____

_____

_____

_____

_____

_____

CHAPTER 3: INSECURITIES

On a scale from 1 to 10, with 10 being the highest, how would you rate your level of insecurity?

_____

_____

_____

_____

_____

_____

_____

_____

_____

_____

_____

Musiq

🎵*How does your man or woman rate your level of insecurity?* 🎵

_____

_____

_____

_____

_____

_____

_____

_____

_____

_____

_____

🎵 *Is it wrong to go through someone's phone records or emails?* 🎵

_____

_____

_____

_____

_____

_____

_____

_____

_____

_____

_____

_____

CHAPTER 4: REDEMPTION

🎵 *When does a person not deserve a second chance?* 🎵

_____

_____

_____

_____

_____

_____

_____

_____

_____

_____

_____

🎵 *Is there a double standard when it comes to men and women and second chances (and if YES, who or what is to blame?)?* 🎵

_____

_____

_____

_____

_____

_____

_____

_____

_____

_____

_____

_____

CHAPTER 5: 142
♪ Who's hit the hardest when it comes to loving one's self, men or women? ♪

_____

_____

_____

_____

_____

_____

_____

_____

_____

_____

_____

🎵 *Is entertainment and society in general responsible for why so many people are unhappy with themselves? And if so, what can be done to change this and better the way men and women relate?* 🎵

_____

_____

_____

_____

_____

_____

_____

_____

_____

_____

_____

CHAPTER 6: SEX

🎵 *Is there a double standard when it comes to men and sex, and if so why?* 🎵

_____

_____

_____

_____

_____

_____

_____

_____

_____

_____

_____

🎵 *How much do you believe gender roles contribute to the perception of sex by men as compared to women?* 🎵

_____

_____

_____

_____

_____

_____

_____

_____

_____

_____

_____

Musiq

🎵 *Are women at all to blame for the way most men go about sex?* 🎵

_____

_____

_____

_____

_____

_____

_____

_____

_____

_____

_____

🎵 *Do women add to the belief that it's cool for a man to sleep around?* 🎵

_____

_____

_____

_____

_____

_____

_____

_____

_____

_____

_____

_____

CHAPTER 7: MONEY

🎵 *Is it still an issue for most men if a woman makes more money?* 🎵

_____

_____

_____

_____

_____

_____

_____

_____

_____

_____

🎵 *Should the man have to pay every time he takes a woman out to dinner?* 🎵

_____

_____

_____

_____

_____

_____

_____

_____

_____

_____

_____

Musiq

🎵 *Is there too much pressure on men to perform when it comes to money, and how does this impact a relationship?* 🎵

_____

_____

_____

_____

_____

_____

_____

_____

_____

_____

CHAPTER 8: FRIENDS & FAMILY

🎵At what point do you think the line should be drawn when it comes to your parents and your relationship? 🎵

_____

_____

_____

_____

_____

_____

_____

_____

_____

_____

_____

_____

Musiq

🎵 *At what point do you think the line should be drawn when it comes to your friends and your relationship?* 🎵

_____

_____

_____

_____

_____

_____

_____

_____

_____

_____

_____

CHAPTER 10 & 11

🎵 Are women held to higher expectations when it comes to marriage material as compared to men? 🎵

_____

_____

_____

_____

_____

_____

_____

_____

_____

_____

_____

Musiq

♩ How do men feel about women with nasty attitudes? And how come some women think that a less than sweet attitude is necessary? ♪

_____

_____

_____

_____

_____

_____

_____

_____

_____

_____

🎵 At what point is the woman to blame if she finds herself as someone's buddy? 🎵

_____

_____

_____

_____

_____

_____

_____

_____

_____

_____

_____

CHAPTER 12: GOOD MAN

🎵 Is it really that hard to find a good man? 🎵

_____

_____

_____

_____

_____

_____

_____

_____

_____

_____

_____

_____

♪ Are women at a disadvantage when it comes to finding a good man? ♪

_____

_____

_____

_____

_____

_____

_____

_____

_____

_____

_____

Musiq

🎵 Are men and women on different pages regarding what they believe makes a man "good"? 🎵

_____

_____

_____

_____

_____

_____

_____

_____

_____

_____

_____

🎵 *How does society, women, and gender roles impact how men in general relate to women?* 🎵

_____

_____

_____

_____

_____

_____

_____

_____

_____

_____

_____

Musiq

LOVE LESSONS

🎵 What things could men do better, or more of, to show greater appreciation for their partner? 🎵

_____

_____

_____

_____

_____

_____

_____

_____

_____

_____

♪ **What things could women do better, or more of, to show greater appreciation for their partner?** ♪

_____

_____

_____

_____

_____

_____

_____

_____

_____

_____

_____

Musiq

🎵 In what ways, typically, are both men and women unrealistic when it comes to their partners? 🎵

_____

_____

_____

_____

_____

_____

_____

_____

_____

_____

_____